Grimaulkin Tales

L. A. Jacob

Published by Paper Angel Press
paperangelpress.com

Cover design copyright © 2019 by Niki Lenhart
nikilen-designs.com

ISBN 978-1-949139-33-4 (Trade Paperback)

10 9 8 7 6 5 4 3 2 1

FIRST EDITION

Dedication

To you, Gentle Reader.
Without You, none of this would be possible.

AUTHOR'S NOTE

The music chosen usually doesn't have anything to do with the lyrics (unless otherwise noted), but the cadence and rhythm of the song. So if you can, strip the vocals from the song and listen to it karaoke style.

CONTENTS

THE DEMON'S TALE

This was the first draft beginning of Grimaulkin. Instead, I separated this story and "Self-Defense", the two most important moments of Mike's life before prison.

This story was originally published in Selections, *an anthology by the Association of Rhode Island Authors (ARIA).*

"DEVIL" by Shinedown

I SUMMONED MY FIRST DEMON WHEN I WAS 12.

That summer, I stayed with my Aunt Jane, who was a witch. I studied some of her books on paganism, but that New Age-y, mushy stuff didn't interest me. I wanted revenge.

Christoforo Arcuri — known ironically as "Mousey", because he was huge — had been beating me up ever since I started school. He tipped my desk over onto me the first time I met him. He beat me up even after I gave him my lunch money. He stole my books and ran around the playground, making me chase after him.

I tried to fight back once, but I was told I "hit like a girl", and got a black eye for my trouble.

Even my older brother Phil got into the act: sometimes just watching, laughing at my antics. Sometimes he'd go up to Mousey and tell him to "cool it" and then he'd retrieve whatever item Mousey had stolen from me. Phil would then constantly remind me of these times whenever a chore came up that he didn't want to do.

It was time to take things into my own hands. If I couldn't fight Mousey on his turf, then I was going to fight him on mine.

He hadn't been studying the hierarchy of demons since he could read. He hadn't gone on Sabbats and rituals with a witch and a coven since he was eight. He didn't know that I knew magic. Nobody knew, except Aunt Jane and Uncle Joey and my sister Evelyn. Evie kept it from Phil and my parents, and would probably let herself be tortured before she ever admitted to anyone that I was a witch. Not a warlock. There's no such thing as warlocks.

I summoned the demon in the middle of the forest that the coven used for rituals. I set up a circle using twigs to show the boundaries. At the four quarters of North, South, West, and East, I lit candles in glass. North had a pile of dirt in front of it. South had a cauldron. West held a cup of spring water. And a censer burned in the East.

I called the demon. Andromalius was white, beautiful, and naked, with a snake curling around him. You will find him in the *Lesser Key of Solomon*.

He spoke without his lips moving, a gentle voice on the wind, "Who summons me?"

"I am Michael," I said, for once glad that I had a powerful name.

The demon looked down at me. His face, his whole countenance was gentle.

"What is your wish, Master?"

Demons were wily, my aunt had warned me, and they often flattered the summoner. I needed to be strong. I had to stick to my purpose.

"You will punish Christoforo Arcuri."

"Who is this man?"

I nodded to the center of the circle. There was a school picture of him that I had cut out from the classroom photo we all took together. I also added the torn-off cover of his Science book that had drawings all over it. I knew I needed both a picture and an essence of him, and that was all I could get my hands on.

The demon turned and went to the items. He stared down at them, studying them.

"Set me free, and I will do as you will."

"No, I will not set you free. You will do as I command and no more. I bind you, Andromalius. I bind you. I bind you."

Each time I said the words, I clapped my hands. It would sound like thunder to the demon, and would tie invisible chains from him to my will. When — and only when — I knew Mousey was taken care of, would I cut the invisible chains in a ritual to unbind him.

Until then, he was mine to do what I wanted.

Andromalius' snake dropped. The demon and snake hissed at me.

"You will punish Christoforo Arcuri. He is a wicked, wicked boy."

"Punish this boy." He flipped the picture over, and caressed the book cover. "Then you will release me."

"Yes," I said, though I didn't say where I was going to release him to.

The snake climbed up Andromalius' leg, and he took the creature in his arms. He stepped forward to me. For a moment, I could see his true form: a large, angry snake. And then he was gone.

I said the required prayer for the dismissal of the circle. A hot breeze momentarily caressed my face. I turned around to see my aunt, sitting at the base of a tree off to the side. I smiled at her.

"I did it."

She struggled to get off the ground. She was short and wide before it became normal for many Americans. She got to her hands and knees and I helped her up the rest of the way.

"Thanks, Mikey." She looked up at the stars and then the moon. "Ah, we'd better get home."

After we cleaned up the area to make it look not used, we started walking the mile or so back to the car.

"How did it feel?" she asked me.

"I could do it. I could do anything!"

She smiled, rustled my hair. "Just be careful, Mikey. What are the Four Pillars?"

"To Know, To Dare, To Will, To Be Silent."

"So we're going to let the spell work on its own."

On the way home, we stopped at a convenience store to pick up some candy.

At her apartment in the assisted-living complex, we walked in to hear Uncle Joey guffaw loudly at the TV. He saw us come in, and switched on the light in the living room, as he liked to watch TV in the dark.

"Hey, hey, how's my little witches?"

"Wonderful!"

Aunt Jane tossed him a candy bar. He caught it on the fly and patted the chair next to him. Aunt Jane took off her coat and said, "He did a great job."

"Did you see it?" Uncle Joey asked, as I went to sit on the couch.

"Uh huh," I said.

"What did it look like?"

I described Andromalius to him as best as I could, and he nodded. He wasn't a witch, but he let Aunt Jane have her way with the pagan stuff. He understood, like Aunt Jane and I did, that demons weren't evil; they were spirits. However, if left to their own devices, they could be malicious and evil. It was up to the magician to teach them and keep them on a tight leash.

And as I described Andromalius, my breath caught. I know my eyes widened. Aunt Jane looked at me.

"What's wrong?"

"I didn't tell it what to do. I said 'punish' him."

Aunt Jane waved a hand. "He won't kill him. They never do, unless you tell them to."

My Aunt Jane was not a believer in the Rule of Three: whatever you do comes back at you three times worse or better. I, even in my young age, believed in something more like the typical Westerner's belief of karma.

I hoped Andromalius didn't kill him. I didn't want to die.

I slept over at Aunt Jane's that night and Phil came to pick me up in the morning. We lived four blocks away from my aunt's high-rise, in our own three-bedroom house just outside of New Haven. Phil was three years older than me, but he was only two grades ahead of me.

He came to the house wearing a t-shirt and shorts, his waistband down to his hips, showing his knit boxer underwear.

"Pull up your pants," my aunt ordered Phil, as she gathered my stuff to bring home. "He's already had lunch."

"'kay," he said, sniffing.

"You want some too?"

"Nah," he said.

"It's lasagna."

Phil got that distant look that meant he was thinking.

"I'll give you some in a container."

As soon as we were out the door, he thrust the lasagna at me. "You carry it," he said, and walked ahead of me, brooding. He was 15. He didn't want me around.

I got home and saw that my father's car was not in the driveway. Phil was already home; I could tell by the cast-off sneakers inside the mudroom. I picked them up for him and placed them on the shelf, then took off my own sneakers.

I smelled baking. It was Sunday, and my mother was cooking for the week. She saw how to do it in one of those women's magazines a few weeks ago and was trying it on us. However, by Wednesday, we were tired of frozen food.

"Hi, mom," I called, and came into the kitchen.

"Hi, Mike. What's that?"

"Lasagna." I handed over the container.

"I doubt it's low-fat," she said with a snort, and tossed it in the garbage.

She and I were about the same height. I was of average weight, but my mother was always getting us to try and lose weight.

"Are you going to clean your room?"

"Yes, mom," I said, slightly dejected.

I always ended up cleaning the bedroom Phil and I shared, but I wanted to cook with her.

She knew it and said, "After you're done, we'll make some cookies."

"Okay!" I went out of the kitchen, into the living room where Phil sat on Dad's recliner, watching some videotaped wrestling. I headed to the stairs.

"Hey," he said to me. I turned around. "Don't forget to pick up the clothes."

I felt like Cinderella.

I carried my backpack upstairs and went to work on the room. After vacuuming, I dusted, picked up the clothes, brought them down to the laundry, and put them in the washer. I made the beds, and then went to join my mother.

She was sitting at the kitchen table, looking through her *Taste of Home* magazines. My father walked in the door just as I said, "Okay, mom!"

He stood in the mudroom, taking off his hat. He was a tall, overbearing man, with a paunch from beer and bread.

"Marge?"

My mother got up as if she was on a leash. All of us kids had learned to do that. Or we got smacked.

"Where's my blowtorch?"

"In the garage," she said.

"It's not where I looked. Didn't I use it last year to peel the paint off the window in Evie's room?"

"I don't think it's there anymore," she said, going over to my father in the hallway. She put her hand on her hip and regarded him. "Maybe you left it in the cellar with the paint."

"I'll check there." He walked by my mother without even a kiss, a hug, or any type of endearment. It wasn't surprising. He also walked by me without acknowledging me and went into the living room.

I turned to my mother expectantly. "What kind of cookies?"

She went back to the magazines. "Here's a recipe. I think we have all the ingredients."

Hershey's Kisses cookies! One of my favorites!

I gathered all the ingredients and started making the cookies while she sat at the kitchen table and smoked, looking through her magazines. This was the best time ever during the week.

My father didn't find his blowtorch, so he had to go to Ace to get a new one. He brought Phil with him because I was still baking cookies.

By the time my dad got back, he was grumpy. I had baked the cookies and was enjoying them when he snapped, "Get outside and come help me."

Disappointed, I got up and went outside. He was setting up a ladder against the garage, with Phil and I watching him. He stared at me as if I was stupid.

"Hold the ladder!" he yelled, and I ran to do his bidding. "Don't pull the rope," he said, carrying the blowtorch and a chisel, and started up the ladder.

Phil leaned against the car, his arms crossed, looking from my father to me. He grinned at me — a malicious grin — and then headed back into the house.

My father saw him go into the house. "Phil!"

Phil peeked out. "Yeah?"

"Get out here. You think I trust your brother?"

Phil came back, his shoulders hunched.

"Hold the ladder," my father ordered him, and he held it on the opposite side.

I held onto the ladder, staring at the rope between us, wondering what would happen if I pulled it. Would my father fall the ten feet to his death? On days like today, that didn't sound too bad.

As he scraped, curls of paint fell on us. We would let go of the ladder to brush them off, then he would yell at us to keep holding the ladder.

Phil glared at me. "This is all your fault. If you weren't such a girl, you could hold the ladder yourself."

"I'm not a girl!" I yelled at him.

"Faggot."

"Jerk."

"Gay faggot."

"Stop it!" yelled my father. "Jesus Christ, I'm almost done."

I held about ninety percent of the time, while Phil just laid his hands on the ladder, looking bored. Finally, the ladder started to shake as my father came down. I held it tighter, and so did Phil. My father pushed past me to get his feet on the ground.

He went back up with a paint bucket this time. We had to hold the ladder until he was done.

"The work is done, Master."

It wasn't a dream.

My eyes snapped open. In the dark of my room, I could see Andromalius, the white snake coiled around his naked body as he stood in the area between my bed and Phil's.

Phil slept like a stone.

"Release me." Andromalius stood, waiting.

I eased out of the bed, and whispered. "Come with me." There was no way I could do a banishment ritual in the middle of my room.

I tiptoed in the dark down the hall, past the living room, and out into the garage. Andromalius followed me like a shade gliding along the floor.

The first thing I did was use chalk to draw a protective circle. That was for me to stay in after I released him, so he wouldn't come after me. Then I drew his circle with his sigil in it, along with the sigils of his three binding angels.

I stepped into my circle and pointed him to his circle. He hesitated. Those three binding angels were what stopped him.

"You will not come after anyone I know or care about?"

"Certainly, Master," he said.

I erased the three angels. He stepped into the circle willingly.

"What did you do to him?" I asked the demon.

"He had a water jet ski accident and is paralyzed from the waist down."

He'd never be back in school again. I couldn't help but smile.

"Cool," I said.

Then I raised my hands and began the prayer that summoned forth the three angels.

"You are to release me!"

The three angels, that actually looked more like white eagles, appeared outside of the circle. Flapping their broad wings, they attacked Andromalius, talons and beaks tearing his spirit apart.

When nothing but the echo of his scream remained, the door to the garage opened and Evie stood in the doorway. "Mikey?"

"Yeah?" I quickly started rubbing away the circles on the ground.

"What're you doing?"

"Nothing," I said. "Practicing."

Summer ended soon enough and Fall came. School started and I went in with some trepidation. Mousey had not arrived the first few days of school, which turned into the first few months. I was free.

Until we came back from December break. As I got on the bus, I sat next to a boy that I always sat next to. The boy never spoke to me. He kept looking out the window, even when I would try to talk to him.

Then, that one day after December break, a bigger boy grabbed me out of the seat and punched me in the ribs. I couldn't breathe.

He threw me to the floor. "I'm sittin' here from now on," he said. "Go somewhere else."

I struggled up, but no one would let me sit next to them. Finally, a girl at the very far back of the bus felt bad and scooted over for me.

So it wasn't just Mousey. It was going to be other kids. More kids. Different kids.

It would never end.

THE ORIGIN TALE

Never tick off a Magician.

This is Mike's "origin story", how he got into prison.

"*Coming Undone*" by Korn (including lyrics)

I GAZED AT CHRIS, WHO GAVE ME A COY SMILE. We had no shirts on. We were getting dressed for gym.

"What're you looking at?" he asked, still with that cute smile. I was only 12, but I had already accepted that girls weren't my thing. Something told me that he thought the same way, too.

I walked up to him. I stared into his black eyes, looked at the black hair framing his face, and then down to his lips. He was breathing in gasps, like those girls in the romances my mother read.

I started to lean forward. This would be my first boy kiss, ever. I would place my lips gently on his, just to feel what it was like, and then —

He screamed, backed up. "You're a fag?"

His shouted question echoed through the empty locker room.

"You were gonna kiss me! You're gross!" Then he bolted out of the locker room area and headed up the stairs.

I stood there, blinking. He hadn't even put on his shirt. I put mine on and then my shorts. *But didn't he — wasn't he — he seemed like —*

I tied my sneakers and went up the stairs. As soon as I cleared the doorway of the locker room, I felt one of the big red rubber balls hit me square in the stomach. I doubled over as one of the other kids grabbed my arm, yanking me hard toward him. He kicked the ball back to someone who kicked it again. This time the ball hit my outstretched arm. The kid let go of me, and I lost my balance, falling backward.

"Mike," said the teacher. "Get over here."

I got to my hands and knees. When the teacher looked away, the kid who grabbed my arm kicked my arm, making me fall again.

"Faggot," he said, walking away.

That's when the chant started.

"Mikey's a faggot. Mikey's a faggot."

The teacher whirled around to face me. I felt like a huge spotlight from heaven pooled around me and that everyone, girls and boys, knew. I felt my face get so hot that I wanted to cry.

The teacher came over to me, and, without touching me, he said, "Go on Jason's team."

"I don't want a faggot on my team," said Jason when I walked up to him.

"Stop saying that," ordered the teacher, and gave me a gentle push toward Jason. The kids parted away from me and looked strangely at me. Chris was on the other team. They were whispering, staring at me.

"Play outfield," said Jason to me. "You're worthless otherwise."

I hung my head. Kickball was never my thing — hell, athletics in general wasn't my thing. I never dove for the ball, sacrificing my body to make the save. Nobody let me catch the ball. Nobody let me kick the ball. It was worse than cooties; it was the Plague.

The rumor spread like the biggest scandal ever in school. I sat alone for lunch. My usual group had gotten up and left me there. People deliberately moved their desks away from me, even if it was a half an inch. Teachers weren't sure what to do. My math teacher sat me in the back corner of the class, as if I was the boy in the bubble.

How did I feel?

Confused at first. My friends weren't coming near me. My enemies were looking at me with grins and probably with knives in their pockets, ready to tear me to ribbons. It was just a rumor, right?

Then I had to get on the bus.

I thought I was going to have a spot all to myself. But the bus was too crowded for that. I took a seat next to Jimmy who had been my friend since third grade. He hugged the window.

Andrew sat next to me. Andrew was a kid who took karate. Surely, he'd protect me.

As soon as a spot became available somewhere else, though, he ran. Then Ryan sat next to me. Ryan was a friend of Mousey's.

"So, you're the faggot."

I didn't say anything. Instead, I looked down at the floor, so he punched me in the side of the head.

"'Ja hear me now, faggot?"

I put my hands up to my head. He punched me next in the gut.

"Fight!" someone yelled, as I tried to make myself as small as I could under the pummeling blows.

It was like I was back in third grade, with Mousey using me as a punching bag every week. I'd come home with bruises and black eyes at least twice a month. Until finally, one day …

Ryan got up, leaving me there, a quivering mass of muscle and bruised bone. The monitor could do nothing but yell, and even that, she wasn't good at. A kid from another grade took Ryan's place. He was bigger, on the junior varsity. He started hitting me, too, mostly in the face. The kids were getting a kick out of it, but I didn't do anything to fight back. I was saving it up.

They would pay. Oh, they would pay.

The monitor said something to the bus driver, who started yelling at kids to stop. It didn't work. My stop was coming up. The monitor knew it, and she came to where I was. As other kids piled off, and the kid who was hitting me moved to another seat, the monitor helped me up.

"C'mon, I'll bring you to the door."

I couldn't see out of one eye; it was cut in my eyebrow somewhere.

"You're gonna get AIDS!" said one of the kids, and that chant started up.

The monitor didn't seem to care as she brought me two doors down from the bus stop directly to my house. The bus driver was beeping the horn to try to get the monitor's attention; the kids were staring out the back window.

"Are you going to be okay?" the monitor asked me.

I nodded. I had left my backpack on the bus, but I didn't care. I was alive, albeit barely.

I felt like I crawled up the lawn to my front door. I didn't have the strength to get to the back door. My hand was swollen as I fished my key out of my pocket. It slipped out and fell to the wooden porch.

That's when I sat down and started to cry.

It didn't last very long, because I thought of how everyone was going to pay for it: the kids on the bus; my father, when he found out; my brother, if he found out. Everyone. Everyone was going to pay for all the things they'd done to me over the years.

I knew what I had to do. I picked up the key and slipped it into the keyhole, turned the knob, and let myself in. I was dizzy, but I used the edge of the door frame to stand up. I stumbled into the house, closing the door behind me.

I made my plans.

As soon as the vertigo left me, I went into my room. I retrieved the backpack that I had for magic items — magical things that my Aunt Jane and I would go on excursions with. I stuffed a gym bag with a couple of changes of clothes, pausing for dizziness to pass.

Then I went back out to the kitchen and down the hall, and to the garage. No one parked a car in the garage, as it stored most of the things we needed for seasonal items: gardening gear, snow gear, Christmas stuff. I moved some things around. I needed a clear space on the floor, at least ten feet wide.

I rummaged around in my backpack, pulling out a thick stick of sidewalk chalk. It was pink, but it would have to do.

I drew a circle on the concrete. Then I concentrated and drew the symbol of the most powerful demon I dared to summon.

Belial, King of Hell.

Next, I drew my protection circle, about four feet in diameter. I gathered my backpack and took out the bottle of spring water I kept in it. I sprinkled the circle, then me with it. I didn't say the incantations, but kept them in mind as I consecrated the circles with a lit candle, a sprinkle of salt, and a soft clap for air. They were all shortcuts, I know. But I knew what I was doing.

I found my *athame*, my magical knife that Aunt Jane gave me for my 10th birthday. I held the athame and began the conjuring. I shouted the words, as your voice goes across the aether to gather the spirit that is required. I knew from experience, when I had summoned my first demon at the age of 12, that it was the force of your will that gathered (or banished) the demon.

Belial appeared, in full armor, trumpets blaring around him. They weren't really blaring; they were in my head. I felt my pains go away. I raised my head up high, looking directly at Belial.

"How may I serve you, Boy Wizard?"

"Kill anyone who's ever hurt me. Keep their souls."

He laughed.

I had to give him a time limit for the contract. "You have one turn of the earth."

"Many people will die."

I thought of Ryan … Chris … Jason … The kid I didn't know on the bus. The teachers. My supposed friends.

I said flatly, "I suppose so."

He put his armored hands up against the boundary of the circle. "Release me."

I bent to the edge of his circle, and dragged the point of the *athame* across the chalk, creating a crack in the circle. The "circle" was actually a sphere that surrounded us, protecting me and keeping him in that sphere. Once I cracked the circle, it was like cracking an egg. He put both hands on the sides of the crack and pulled, opening the sphere wide.

As soon as he stepped through it, he disappeared.

I cut my protective circle with a downward swipe of my *athame*. I smelled the rusty iron of Belial's armor on the air.

Next, I got my bike down from its rack. I rolled it out into the mudroom, then out onto the lawn. With the tie-downs on my bike, I put my gym bag on the back. I wore the backpack. I was planning on riding to my Aunt Jane's house, about an hour away. From there, I would run away, or maybe come back later, since most of the town would be dead.

I heard a car pull into the driveway, and saw Phil, my brother, at the wheel. He threw open his door and yelled at me: "You!"

My aches and pains had gone away, so I could jump on my bike.

"It's true, isn't it?" Phil shouted from the car. "You're a faggot."

I didn't say anything. I only looked at him and thought, *Anytime now, Belial.*

"No brother of mine's a faggot!" He got out of the car and started to run at me.

I was on the bike, and could have ridden away, and almost did. Then he stopped. His eyes widened, and he fell face-first onto the lawn, arms at his sides, as if he had been merely standing straight and got pushed over onto the grass. He fell hard.

I didn't stick around.

I kept punching in Aunt Jane's number on the phone outside of the high-rise building she lived in. She finally picked up the third time I called.

"Hello?" she said, out of breath.

"Aunt Jane, I'm in trouble."

"Mikey?"

"Yeah."

"What's wrong, honey?"

"Can you come downstairs and get me?"

I had hidden my bike by the railroad tracks next to the high-rise. I didn't care if someone happened upon it and decided to take it. I was going to be far away by the time Aunt Jane knew what was going on at my house.

Aunt Jane came downstairs to the door of the high-rise and let me in. The place stunk of old cigarettes and urine. She burned incense constantly, to ongoing the consternation of her neighbors. She put a hex on one of them and he died a few weeks later. Coincidence? We didn't think so.

She was a heavyset woman with swollen legs and feet. She couldn't walk much, and when we went into the woods for our magical rites, she couldn't really get around very well. I helped her the best I could.

"What's happened?" she asked me. She didn't seem that concerned.

"I killed someone, I think."

"Who?"

"Phil."

Her eyes widened at that. "Let's go upstairs."

I must have looked fine, because she didn't comment on how battered and bruised I had looked before. Belial and his energy had kindly healed me before going out and harvesting souls.

We took the elevator to the 9th floor. As we exited the elevator, I could hear a woman screaming at someone to shut up. A baby was crying behind another door. Aunt Jane walked past the chaos behind each of the doors to her corner apartment, and opened it, letting me in. The smell of burnt sandalwood assaulted me, overwhelming the scent of hopelessness from the hall.

She gave me a lemonade and a chocolate pudding cup, and I told her what happened.

"New Haven's going to be all full of dead people by tomorrow night," I said. "My father, Phil, all the kids in school …"

"Phil might not be dead," said Aunt Jane.

"I know he is."

She sighed. "We should banish Belial, or he will be a spirit on the loose, destroying people you don't want destroyed." Aunt Jane called them spirits, not demons. But I knew them for what they were. "Tonight, at midnight, summon him back and tell him that you've changed your mind. He's going back now."

"How fast can he kill people?"

"It depends. If — *if* — he killed Phil in the split second it took for him to get from the car to you, then it could be seconds. Minutes."

"The town will be dead."

"Not everyone."

"All the kids!"

She sighed again. "It's very dangerous to summon a spirit and give him *carte blanche* like that."

"Carte blanche?"

"Free reign." She sat down. "We'll go to our usual spot in the woods and hopefully there won't be any kids there drinking tonight."

Nobody called her to tell her that Phil was dead, and she wasn't going to call to find out. We had dinner, and then waited up until midnight. I had passed out on the couch at 9, and she woke me up at 11:30.

"It's time," she said. She wore her magical robes and walked with a willow staff.

I got up and followed her out the door.

We stepped outside into the coolness of the night air, and headed to her car. Suddenly, three black vans came screaming into the parking lot, one stopping just short of Aunt Jane. The doors burst open and men flowed out, one man grabbing her, knocking her staff to the ground.

"Auntie!" I yelled, as two men from behind me grabbed me and whipped me around. I struggled out of my jacket, and out of their arms. I took off in between two vans, slamming shut one of the doors as I ran past it.

I wove between cars in the parking lot. If I could get to the railroad tracks, I could outrun them there. I didn't know who these guys were, but they were dangerous.

I squeezed through a fence and slid down the embankment to the railroad tracks. My bike was still there. I didn't have time to retrieve it. My feet hit the gravel and I started to pour on the speed, running up the tracks.

Then someone tackled me, and we both slid along the wood and steel of the rail. I slammed my head against the rail and saw stars. My arms were yanked behind my back, and I heard the click of cuffs around my wrists. Whoever caught me hauled me to my feet.

I looked into the gray eyes of my captor. They were cold, unseeing, dead. Then he pushed me off the tracks, into the gravel that lined the side of it. We started walking back to the high-rise. I said nothing, knowing my Miranda rights from watching too much "*Law and Order*".

Forced up the embankment, someone grabbed me by my shirt and hauled me through the cut in the fence. I dug in my heels so they had to literally drag me to one of those black vans. They tossed me in the back — at least it was carpeted — and slammed shut the doors, leaving me in darkness.

Then the van started to move. I wondered what happened to Aunt Jane, and who the hell these guys were. But most of all, where were they taking me?

I wasn't secured in the back, so I ended up rolling around as they took a few turns, barely missing the bottom of the metal bench that the van had on each side. After the rolling around stopped, I realized that they must have been on a straight-away, or a highway.

The sound of the van was muffled in here, but the carpeting smelled new. I inched my way up to the back — or front — of the van, away from the doors, and managed to get into a sitting position. I wondered if they did the same thing to Aunt Jane — poor Aunt Jane, who could barely get around *without* both hands tied behind her back.

My hands hurt, then went numb after a while. I wracked my brain to try and figure out who these people were. Were they the government? Aunt Jane didn't tell me anything about the government and witchcraft.

One thing I didn't do was cry. As I sat in the back, I was more worried about Aunt Jane, and angry about my situation. It seemed hours before the van stopped and they opened the doors.

It was, in fact, hours. It was still before sunrise, because I could see the rest area lit up, even though the area around was light enough to see the gray outline of things. However, the men who dragged me out were all in black with sunglasses, looking not unlike the "Blues Brothers" or "Men in Black".

Without a word, they led me into the bathroom, unzipped my fly and stood over me as I did my business.

"What's going on?" I asked them. "Who are you?"

They didn't answer me as they fixed me up and then dragged me out to the van. They unceremoniously tossed me back inside it. It took a little while, long enough for me to get back to my sitting position, before we were back on our way.

The next time they stopped and pulled me out of the van, it was full day. I blinked in the brightness, and looked at where I was.

Before me was a huge stone structure, with towers on either end of it. The windows were small, set high on one end, with normal, larger windows on the other end. A set of black doors about ten feet high stood in front of me. They opened as the two men flanking me stepped into the building.

I looked at the ceiling and could see magical runes etched and painted in the dome above. I heard the doors close behind me, and they finally unlocked my cuffs. I rubbed at my hands to try and get the feeling back in them. They shoved me to the right, down a long hallway.

A door was open and a man in what looked like ancient Roman gear stood there, holding a spear. He pointed the spear at me, its tip at my heart. All the guys behind me had to do was push me forward and I'd be impaled.

Instead, the tip of the spear seemed to tickle me, and I felt goosebumps across my chest. He removed the spear and the two men behind me stepped forward. They opened a pair of six-foot tall mahogany doors and thrust me inside the room beyond them, then quietly shut the door behind me.

I was now in a room that looked very much like an English courtroom. I was in a boxed-in area with a bench to the side, facing the front of the room. To my right were two tables and four chairs, all of them full of men. They weren't in powdered wigs and robes, but normal suits. One of the men was the one who had caught me.

Seated at the front of the room were three men in black robes. Obviously judges, they scrutinized me carefully. Beyond them was not a flag, but a tapestry of a cross with a Tudor rose in its center. It suddenly occurred to me who these people were.

Rosicrucians.

These Knights of the Rosy Cross were not too much unlike the Freemasons, but they used and performed magic in the name of God. The Knights Templar were associated with them at one point. At least that's what I could find out through AOL.

The judge in the center, a man with a gray handle-bar mustache and thickly chiseled face, said to someone at the back of the room, "He has been neutralized?"

"Yes, your honor," said the man in the Roman armor.

"Michael Robert LeBonte," said the judge on the farthest right, a man with tousled black hair and a rounded face. "You summoned the demon Belial, did you not?"

I gulped. "Yes — yes, sir."

"Who told you to summon the demon?"

"Nobody did."

"Not your teacher?"

"No. I summoned the demon myself."

"You're how old?"

"I'll be thirteen this weekend."

The man who had caught me said, "Old enough to know right from wrong."

The judges nodded. Said the judge in the middle, "What do you know about Belial?"

"He's a King of Hell, has seventy-two Legions —"

"Enough," said the judge on the farthest left. "He knows right from wrong, and is familiar with the demon. He should have known that what he did was illegal."

Well, I suspected having a demon kill people was pretty illegal.

"He also took flight, knowing that what he had done was illegal."

None of the four men below were coming to my defense.

I said, "Hey, don't I have a right to an attorney?"

"Since you performed the deed, you must defend yourself," said the middle judge. "Do you know where you are?"

"In a court," I said. "I haven't gotten my rights read to me." I knew some people got let off on that technicality.

"You have no rights," declared the middle judge. "You are not in a mundane courtroom, but a court set up specifically for wizards and witches who cross the line and cause havoc in the mundane world."

"You released a demon from Hell into the mundane world," said the judge on the right. "And gave it an open-ended command so that it could do anything."

The left-hand judge said to the four men, "Pathfinder, how many souls did it harvest before we banished it?"

"Nine, Your Honors," said a blond man who was next to the man who had captured me.

The middle judge turned to face me. "Nine souls destined for another life, who have been harvested into the legions of Belial."

The left-hand judge said, "I'm sure it would have been more if the Knights did not find the demon. You told the demon 'everyone'."

The right-hand judge made a steeple of his fingers and stared at me. "He may have been put up to this by his teacher."

"His teacher has stated that she didn't know anything about this," said another man in black sitting among the four at the table. "We interrogated her thoroughly."

"What did you do to her?" I demanded. Now I was angry.

No one answered my question at that time, conveniently ignoring me. The three judges each wrote something on a small piece of paper, and handed it toward the middle judge. He took the papers, glanced at them, nodded, and turned to me.

"You have been found guilty of summoning a demon of Hell to the Earthly realm. Your punishment is to be determined at the William F. Blackstone prison."

"Prison?" The door behind me opened. "I need to call my family! You can't just put me away!"

The man in Roman armor — or maybe it was a different man in Roman armor, I don't remember at this point — put a hand on my shoulder.

"Ritter," said a judge before I was led away, "You will keep us informed."

"I did it in self-defense!" I screamed, as they yanked me out of the courtroom.

THE TALE OF THE
EIGHT DEATHS

In Grimaulkin, *the first book of the "Grimaulkin" series, and in "Self Defense", it's mentioned that eight people died, including his brother in "Self Defense". This is the story of how the other seven people died, and the death of the one who inadvertently got him in this mess in the first place.*

"45" by Shinedown and "N.W.O." by Ministry

P ETER SHUFFLED THE CARDS, not looking at the three boys he
was playing against. He knew that they were going to wipe
the table with him if he won again; he had seen what they
haddone to the boy on the bus.

"C'mon, man. Deal," snapped Julian.

"Shut up," said Kyle. "He's gotta shuffle 'em good."

Jimmy, the last one, didn't say anything. He had seen
Julian beat up the kid within an inch of his life, and he wasn't
going to rile Julian up, either.

Peter dealt the five-card stud and put out a nickel.

Julian licked his teeth like he did when he was thinking.
Poker could be a complicated game for him, which was why
Peter often won.

Jimmy folded without even putting down his nickel. Kyle grinned and raised. Julian humphed and called. Peter folded, knowing better.

Kyle put out a pair of eights. That beat Julian's hand of nothing.

The game went on like this, with Julian losing steadily, and getting more and more pissed off. Peter could see him seething, playing aggressively, and trying to get his money back.

Within an hour, Julian had lost all the money he came in with — five dollars. The object of his wrath for once was not Peter, but Kyle.

Julian went all-in on the last hand, and Kyle took it away with three of a kind against Julian's pair of tens.

"Son of a bitch!" Julian screamed. Peter and Jimmy winced.

"C'mon, man, it's only a game." Kyle counted his pile of nickels and dimes.

"That's my fucking money."

"Not anymore. You lost it."

"Fuck you," he said, jumping up. Then he tilted his head. "Did you hear that?"

"Hear what?" asked Peter.

"Somebody calling me."

"I don't hear nothin' but your money in my pocket," said Kyle, with a laugh.

Peter whirled his head to face Kyle. Was he honestly trying to push Julian into beating him up? Was he crazy?

Julian left the table, a confused look on his face. Peter took the cards and shuffled them once before stuffing them in his backpack. "I better go home."

"You still have money left. Let me take it off your hands."

Peter shook his head. "Nah. I'd like to keep it."

"Suit yourself."

Peter gathered his coins into a small sack that he carried in his backpack. He got up, and headed for the door —

— just as Julian opened it.

"Oh, hey —"

"Move," Julian said, waving the gun in his hand.

It didn't register that Julian had a gun — a real gun — but the movement did and Peter stepped aside. Julian walked into the living room and pointed the gun at Kyle.

"Oh, man, put that fucking thing down."

Julian pulled the trigger. Nothing happened. He turned the gun around and stared down its barrel.

The sound of the gun's discharge deafened the area. The shot exploded the back of Julian's head. Jimmy screamed like a girl. Peter got bits of skull and brain on his face as he screamed, too.

Kyle stared at Julian as he pitched backward and fell at Peter's feet. Blood started to form in a pool where Julian's head used to be.

"Ohmygod, ohmygod ..."

Kyle whispered a prayer, while Jimmy still screamed. He finally put his hands on his mouth to stop himself, but he whimpered instead.

Then Julian got up.

The three boys stared as Julian turned his body to the right, his hand still on the gun, and he hauled himself up, head blown to pieces, one eye trying to focus on the room. Julian turned and faced Peter. That one eye rolled in the back of Julian's head, but he was facing Peter. Peter put up his hands in surrender.

The gun went off again, this time in Peter's chest. The bloom of red on his Slipknot t-shirt seemed to match the decal. Peter didn't fall at first, but stumbled backwards. He grabbed a hold of the door frame, but slipped and fell into the kitchen.

The body that was Julian turned and faced Kyle. Jimmy screamed again, and went to his knees, putting his arms over his head.

"Julian, hey, man, I'll give you the money back."

The laugh that came from the body gurgled with blood. He held the gun right to Kyle's third eye. Kyle swallowed, and he hoped for another misfire.

Jimmy stopped screaming when Kyle's head exploded. Jimmy had fainted.

"Fish … in a barrel …" Julian gurgled, and shot Jimmy in the neck. At least that would be fun to watch bleed out.

But Julian didn't get to see it, falling face-first into Kyle's body, taking the table with him, spilling all the coins on top of them.

"Henry, take out Tiny."

Henry Blake sighed and looked at the mongrel cocker spaniel in its cage. Why couldn't she take him out? She was probably drunk again and couldn't get off the couch.

His attention was drawn back to the game he was playing on TV.

"Henry!"

"Lemme get this level, ma!"

"Now, dammit!"

Yep, drunk again. Henry pressed a button to pause the game, then heaved himself up from the edge of the bed. The dog was ugly, and stupid to boot.

"C'mon, you dumb dog," he said, as the animal stood up when he did.

It turned around and around in its tight cage, tail wagging, tongue lolling out excitedly. Henry took the leash down from its perch, and the dog seemed to go wild in the cage.

Henry opened the cage, and the dog dashed out—or meant to, but Henry caught him roughly by the collar and yanked him back. He hooked the leash onto its collar. Tiny, a medium-sized dog with a lot of strength, tugged hard on the leash to pull Henry across the room to the door.

Henry risked a glance into the living room.

Yep, his mother sat on the couch, drinking another glass of wine. Probably was feeling no pain at this moment. It was only three-thirty in the afternoon. She usually started around noon and didn't stop until way after he went to bed.

Tugging the dog roughly away from the door, he fought his way outside and out into the driveway. Maybe he could just take him for a poop in the back yard and be done with it.

Tiny would have none of it, though, and went out toward the street.

"Aw, come on," Henry moaned, as he let the dog lead him out to the sidewalk. They lived in a condo area just outside of town.

Henry stopped for Tiny at a couple of places for him to whizz on the poles. He finally did take a dump on someone's lawn. Henry didn't bother to clean it up.

He was at the edge of the condos, facing the small copse of woods that buffered them from the busy street. He turned away, heading back to the house, when he thought he heard a low growl. He turned back, and heard the growl again.

Tiny was growling, while he faced the trees, the hackles on his neck standing up straight.

"What's the matter?" Henry pulled on Tiny, but the dog stood his ground and would not budge.

Henry swore, and tugged the dog again. When he did, he heard a crash in the underbrush, and turned to face the woods as a large Rottweiler came bounding out.

Tiny gave a yelp. Henry dropped the leash as the dog tackled him. It foamed at the mouth, its eyes wild. The Rottweiler clamped on Henry's throat and tore it out. Tiny dashed away, as Henry gurgled on his own blood.

Hank settled back on the couch. He really wanted a beer, but the wife had tossed out most of the liquor in one of her cleaning fits. She decided to go organic, and there was no such thing as organic beer. At least as far as he knew.

He flipped through the channels. A hundred channels, and no games. He found ESPN, but it had just guys talking about sports, no games. He didn't care about the talking heads—he wanted football.

The wife glanced up from her knitting, saw the channel, and sighed. "Is that all you ever watch?"

"It's the only good thing on."

"*Columbo* is on 35."

"I don't wanna watch some cop show."

Click, click, as she knitted. "How were the kids on the bus today?"

"Some kid got his ass kicked."

She looked up. "What happened?"

"How the hell do I know? He was all beat up. We dumped him at his house."

"Did you even check on him?"

"Dottie was all worried, but it wasn't that big of a deal."

Click, click. It was going to drive him crazy.

"What the hell you knitting, anyway?"

"A blanket for Rita's granddaughter."

"You're gonna give it away?"

"Well, yes."

"Why give it away? You gotta pay for the yarn and the time it takes knitting and all that."

"It's a gift." She stopped clicking and put the needles down. "You don't understand because you don't give gifts."

"Why should I?"

"You haven't given me a gift in years."

He leered at her. "I married you, didn't I?"

She glared at him. "I'm going upstairs."

"Go ahead."

She got up. She looked at the needles in her hands. "How much is your life insurance policy?" she asked suddenly.

"From work? I dunno, maybe ten grand, why?"

"Just curious."

She went into the kitchen instead of upstairs.

"Hey, make me a sandwich, will ya?"

"Sure, honey," she called back.

Talking heads. Boring. He switched around and found a war movie on the History Channel. Now this was something he could get into.

A few minutes later, she came back, smiling with a plate and, of all things, an ice-cold beer bottle in her hand.

"Where did you get that?"

"Back of the fridge. I must have missed one." She set both items down on the coffee table in front of him. "Enjoy."

Ah, this was the life.

He picked up the sandwich and bit into it. Ham and cheese with a little too much French's mustard, but hey, she wasn't perfect. He picked up the beer and downed half of it. It tasted kind of funny, but it was probably old after sitting in the back of the fridge for so long. He downed the rest before finishing the sandwich.

He smacked his lips as he settled into the sandwich. He watched TV for a couple of hours, and then went upstairs to bed.

The wife left him for the couch some time in the middle of the night because he snored so loud.

Then he suddenly stopped snoring and went cold.

His wife called 9-1-1 the next morning when he didn't come down for breakfast. After the body was removed, she called the life insurance company.

Alex hitched his backpack over his shoulder and walked along the tracks. Trains never came by these rusty old tracks.

The bridge was fenced off, but he squeezed through the spot cut in the fence to get on the bridge.

The river that flowed beneath was shallow but rough at this time of year. He did what he usually did every time he crossed the bridge: He jumped on the ties, because there was sometimes gaping holes between the ties that dropped to the river below.

He thought fleetingly about the faggot kid on the bus. Alex was the one who called him a faggot, because he hated them. The kid didn't say he wasn't. And he didn't fight back. He was worse than a girl —

Alex tripped, but righted himself, scraping his hands on the wooden slats between the ties.

He looked down between the ties. The river flowed fast and rough.

Then he heard the metal singing.

He lifted his head, confused. Coming down the tracks was a locomotive, a freight train's engine. It would stop at the fence on the other side, Alex knew.

The singing grew louder, and the metal railroad ties shook. He heard the whistle of the engine as it came barreling down the track. It crashed through the fence.

Alex had nowhere to go except down.

Alex rolled over, off the track, thinking he had enough room to clear the engine.

He didn't.

He rolled off the bridge with a scream, into the rushing water below.

They never found his body.

Jane Fisher looked from one man in black to the other while she sat in the back of the van.

"Where are you taking me?"

No answer from the men in black. At least they let Jane sit up in a seat, though her hands were bound by thick hemp rope that scratched her wrists.

Jane looked at the men in black. Two sat on either side of her, both of them holding her arms tightly enough to bruise. Two more sat in the front of the van: one man driving, the other glancing back at her every once in a while.

"Who are you?"

The man in the front passenger seat turned to her. "You should know."

"I don't! Please, tell me."

The man snorted and turned around to face the front.

Jane tried to lift her hands up to wipe her tears, but they shoved her arms down onto her lap. Her tears fell down her cheeks. "Please tell me!"

The van jerked to a stop after a while, and the door slid open. They pulled her out of the van. Jane could smell woods, a bit of pine.

The men in black dragged her away from the van, into the woods, following what seemed to be a rabbit trail. She stumbled, but they held her up and crashed through the woods to a flat area in the middle of some trees.

She could see the pyre in the moonlight. A long stick stood out from the middle of it.

Jane dug in her heels. This time they did drag her, screaming and fighting, over to the pyre. They tried to tie her to the pole. She pulled her arm free and socked one of the men in the face. One of the men grabbed her head and yanked it back, tying her by the neck to the stake.

"Pleaaaaaaaase!" she begged, crying.

"Do you deny teaching a child how to summon Belial?" came a voice to her left.

She turned her head to see another man in black, wearing a 1930's detective's gray hat.

"I taught my nephew — he read the *Key of Solomon*. I didn't teach him."

"Yet you exposed him to it."

"He picked it up. I had it. I never used it. I never taught him anything from there. I'm a pagan!"

"You know the demon he summoned. The demon said you were there."

"Belial. Mikey was being bullied. He needed to do something."

"So you admit to teaching him magic?"

"I showed him paganism. I'm a pagan. I'm a witch!"

"You taught a magician to summon a demon." He made a motion.

Heat started at her feet.

"Wait! I didn't. He did it himself!"

"He wouldn't have done it without you."

"Yes, he could have, he could have!" She couldn't move her feet, as the heat started to become unbearable. Her legs moved, but her feet were in the middle of the fire. "Staaaaaaahhhhp!"

"You are a witch. You taught a child to summon a demon and let it loose to kill."

"No! NO! I didn't! He did it, he did it!"

She kept repeating herself, as the fire caught her clothes, licking her skin.

She screamed, "I'm sorry!"

"Too late for that," said the man, walking away.

She kept screaming, until the screams became full of water, and finally stopped.

Ritter turned to the men surrounding the burning stake.

"Salt the earth when it's ashes."

THE KNIGHT'S TALE

What I wish would have happened to my husband instead of what actually did happen.

"Until the Day is Done" by R.E.M.

REVEREND JAMES BAUER RODE HIS MOTORCYCLE seemingly haphazardly down the highway. He'd been riding bikes since his early teens, knew the rules of the road — but he was running late for a wedding — and, of course, they couldn't start without him.

Why did they have to do it by the seashore? he wondered again, passing a truck on the left. Finding himself snarled behind some slow-speeders in the high-speed lane, he had to pass a car on the right.

He had the bad feeling seconds before the car in front broadsided him.

Bauer woke with something down his throat. He lifted his arm to try and dislodge it, but it was firmly in place.

"Shit, he's awake."

Mere moments later, he felt bliss.

He thought he saw a light at the end of a tunnel.

"Oh, no, it's heaven."

He recoiled from the light. But it came closer to him.

He raised his hand to shield his eyes, to try and see beyond it.

"Not yet," he said. "Please, not yet, God. I have too much to do."

He waited, caught in a dark cocoon, floating in nowhere, no sense of time passing.

"God?"

No answer.

A squeeze on his hand.

He couldn't respond. He tried to will his hand to squeeze back. He thought he could hear voices, just beyond where he lay in the cocoon. He raised his arms, brought together in prayer.

"Please, God, please, let me wake up."

"Shit, he's awake" couldn't be the last thing he would hear in his life.

The voices faded, disappearing, and the squeezing on his hand ended.

"God help me."

He already was a pastor. What else was he supposed to do? How else could he dedicate his life to God?

A gentle voice came to him. Not God. Jesus, maybe. "Jim. Can you hear me?"

"Yes, I can hear you."

"I can't hear you, but listen. I can help you. It'll hurt. You'll be in pain, but you must take an oath to God. Do you hear me?"

Bauer tried to pull at the cocoon with his hands. His hands came away with sticky thin strings. He was going to have to dig.

Every once in a while, he would hear Jesus call to him.,
"You will have to go through hell to get to heaven."
"Please hear me! Yes!"
Then he felt the pain throughout his body.
He squeezed his hand shut, gripping something soft.
It hurt like hell.

Strangely, nothing was broken. Bauer's muscles had fallen into disuse, so he had to go to physical therapy to relearn how to work his muscles again.

To never forget the days, he kept a calendar by his bedside and marked the day that passed every night. Two months had passed when a pair of men in black suits came in.

He walked without aid now, but he still had the walker for longer distances. He could lift twenty pounds without help, and do fifteen sit-ups before tiring.

Bauer looked over the two men, who nodded to him. "Reverend Bauer," one said.

Bauer's mouth dropped. It was the gentle voice that spoke to him in his cocoon. "You."

He nodded. "Yes. I am a Confessor."

"What's that?"

"I see and speak to your soul." He motioned to the other man. "We're with the Rosicrucians. We are a sect of the Christian Church that uses magic and stops evil magicians from possibly summoning evil entities."

Bauer blinked. "Whaaaat?"

The man with the gentle voice chuckled. "I know that's a lot to take in. Let me explain."

He took a chair and hooked it around. The other man went to the window and stood in front of it.

"We heard about your accident. We sent a healer here to mend your broken bones and your body."

"A healer? Like …"

"A healer. Like nothing else."

Bauer touched his chest. "Was anything damaged?"

"Everything was. We helped you after you got out of surgery." The Confessor motioned with his hand toward Bauer's body. "You could have died in hours if we hadn'd saved you."

"God …"

The Confessor nodded. "Yes, He had everything to do with this. It just so happened we were in the area for another reason, and we heard from our Pathfinder that you were injured. A Pathfinder finds people."

"Your Pathfinder found me?"

"Our Pathfinder saw you come in. He called us."

Bauer turned to the other man. "Are you my healer?"

"No," said the man. "I'm a Knight."

The Confessor said, "A Knight is the man in the front line. You were in the National Guard for two years before becoming a pastor, if I'm not mistaken."

Bauer narrowed his eyes. "How do you know —?"

"I know your soul. I know its past. A Knight is like … a soldier. He does the hard work." The Confessor sat back. "And that's why we're here."

Said the man at the window, "A Knight works for the Glory of God. We are His sword and wrath, as well as His compassion and mercy."

"The Knight would guard the world from evil men." "And women."

Bauer put his hand up. "Look, this is an awful lot to —"

"Of course."

The Confessor stood up while the Knight walked in front of the bed Bauer sat on. The Confessor took out a business card and handed it to Bauer.

"Call that number if you're interested. Tell them Samuel came here to talk to you."

Bauer took the card and set it on the bed.

"We'll leave you to your rest. Thank you for your time."

Bauer watched them leave. He was alone in the room. He looked up at the ceiling.

"God, did You send them?"

Did he really expect an answer?

Bauer counted the days since the Rosicrucians came. He prayed for guidance. Without any answer from God, he picked up the phone and called the number.

"Hello?" said the man's voice.

"Samuel came and talked to me."

"One moment, please."

This is silly —

"Yes, hello, Reverend Bauer."

Bauer took a deep breath. "What do I need to do to be a Knight?"

"You take an Oath to assist the Rosicrucians in their fight against evil magicians."

"I'll do that." He owed them that much, for giving him his life.

"Don't think that this is because we saved you," said the Confessor. "We would have let you live your life if you chose."

"I want to be a soldier of God."

"Then you have already taken the Oath in your heart. We will come by in three days."

August 1.

The moment he turned the page on the calendar to Lammas Day, he heard his hospital door open.

Two men walked in carrying a guitar case. Bauer stared at the case. "What's in there?"

"The sword you will swear your Oath on."

"A sword?"

The Confessor set the guitar case on the bed Bauer had vacated. "It's less innocuous in a guitar case than in a scabbard." He unlatched the case and pushed it open.

A gleaming silver sword sat cushioned in red silk and satin. The Confessor used a red silk handkerchief and took it out of the case, holding it horizontally.

"Hold your hands out, palms up."

Bauer did, looking strangely at the Confessor. The Confessor slipped the sword onto his palms.

It felt a lot lighter than he had expected.

"Now what?"

"Say what is in your heart."

Bauer closed his eyes. "I want to be a soldier of God — a Knight."

So shalt thou be, stated a woman's melodious voice.

Bauer snapped open his eyes to focus on the sword.

Thy name is Ritter.

"The sword —"

The Confessor smiled. "What did She say?"

"My name is Ritter."

"You're German?"

"Yes."

"'Ritter' means 'Knight' in German."

Said the Knight, "So She has named you, so you shall be named Ritter."

"Look in the sword. You'll see your face reflected in it."

He looked, and saw his eyes were lighter than the brown they had originally been.

Now they were gray.

"Your Oath has been accepted," said the Knight. "Welcome to The Rosicrucians."

THE INMATE'S TALE

In prison, the old teach the young … and sometimes the other way around.

Available out in the wild for free, "The Inmate's Tale" was originally published as "The Joint" as a freebie, but is included here for completeness.

"Guilty" by Gravity Kills

"YOU CAN'T WRITE ANYTHING DOWN," said James to the new prisoner.

Prisoner 150413 stood five-five, and probably weighed a hundred-twenty pounds soaking wet. His blond hair was messy, as if he had used his fingers to comb through it. He wore the same gray prison uniform as everyone else.

"They'll take whatever you write away."

150413 hung his head down and hugged himself.

James, one of the oldest wizards in the prison, asked, "What's your name?"

"Mike."

"Is that what you want to be known as? Names have power."

"I dunno." 150413 shrugged.

James tapped the prisoner's number tag embroidered on his uniform. "That's your name in here. Remember that names have power."

"What's your name?"

"050756."

150413 nodded. "What are you here for?"

"That's an important question. That'll give you power, too." James rubbed his bare chin. "I'm not sure I should tell you. You're too young to understand."

150413 lifted his head in a gesture of defiance. "I summoned a demon," he said, as if daring James.

"Which one?"

"Belial."

James snorted. "You? You're too young for that."

"I did," 150413 stated. He looked like he was going to stomp his foot for emphasis, but James knew that would be showing the boy's true age. "What happens if I do magic here?"

"Try it and see what happens. But you won't live through it." James motioned around the open room they sat in. "There's runes and wards all over the place that neutralizes your magic. Anyway, if the guards catch you, you go into the Hole."

150413 looked like he wanted to ask about the Hole, but someone came over. Her salt-and-pepper hair was tied back in a ponytail, her light coffee-colored face deeply wrinkled. She shuffled, not walked, to stand before James.

"Baba," he said with a nod to her.

Baba glanced at 150413. "You're new here."

"Yes, ma'am."

Baba cackled. "So polite. You'll lose that in a year."

150413 blanched. "Will I be here that long?"

"Longer," said James. "At least a year for summoning a demon." James thumbed at 150413 and spoke to Baba. "He summoned Belial."

"Times have changed," Baba said, looking 150413 up and down. "They're getting younger."

"You believe him?"

"Why else would he be here with us?"

James only frowned. He didn't believe the boy. He was far too young to actually summon a demon as powerful as Belial. If they were in the outside world, he would ask him to prove it. Here, he couldn't, not without setting off the wards.

"Why are you here?" 150413 asked Baba. He had his hands at his sides, something James read as his guard being down. Just because she was a witch did not mean she wasn't here for a good reason.

"Bathing in the blood of babes." Baba grinned at him.

150413 blinked, brought his arms in closer.

Good, thought James. *Get yourself protected.*

"Seriously?"

"I wanted immortality. I had a spell, and that's what I did. Killed children and bathed in their blood. Looked 25. Until they took the blood away from me."

He swallowed, stared at the woman still grinning at him. She had all her teeth, perfectly white and straight.

"How — how long have you been here?"

"Ah," she said, looking up at the ceiling. "A long, long time."

Someone blew a whistle. The boy jumped. James slowly rose, mostly because his legs didn't work as fast as they used to. "Time to go in, kid."

Everyone got into a line. James stood behind 150413. They were close enough to not touch, but James felt the heat of the boy's aura. He was a sensitive, and the wards didn't stop him from seeing the aura if he wanted to.

James unfocused his eyes and looked at the top of the boy's head. The aura was dark, almost black with white speckles, like distant stars in a night sky. Some of the speckles were tinged red or pink, others gold.

There was some hope for him.

⁂

The next time James saw the boy, 150413 was huddled in the corner, shaking like a rabbit. He and Baba debated on going over to him, but James felt sorry for the boy. He was too young to be put in the general population of witches and wizards, all of them at least ten years older than the boy.

Finally, James gave in and approached him. James saw that one of the guards was watching the boy closely. As soon as James approached, the guard turned away.

"150413," James said to the boy. James saw the boy's shoulders rise, relaxing just a little. "Why are you here in the corner?"

"Him." He nodded toward the group gathered in the other corner, playing craps with dice and imaginary money.

James knew them as the Satanists, a gang of young men and women who celebrated Black Masses. Most of them were in their early 40's now, having been picked up at the height of the Satanic Panic in the '80's. If they renounced their belief in Satan and returned to God, they would be released. These were the diehards.

They were also extremely violent, and it was no wonder that the boy was scared.

"Which one?"

"Malachi."

One of the leaders, Malachi was a bald, tattooed creature who usually beat the newcomers until he got tired of it. James wouldn't be surprised if the boy was covered in bruises under the gray uniform.

"You have to stand up to him," said James, crouching next to the boy. "He only understands fists and fury." However, the boy was small. He wouldn't last.

"This is worse than school," the boy said. "At least I had somewhere to run."

"Which is why you have to stand and fight."

The boy rubbed his nose. "I don't know how."

"A lot of us had to fight here. I'm old, but there are young men here who can teach you." James glanced at the men playing after one of them roared at winning. "You need to gain their respect."

"How?"

"Fight. Don't let them use you."

"So I have to fight in order to learn how to fight?"

"Generally."

The boy bowed his head, looking more dejected. James wanted to put his hand on the boy's shoulder. No, it wouldn't do to get attached to the boy. It would be a weakness here in the prison, and he had survived too many years to show he wasn't weak.

Malachi turned to face them. The boy shook again.

"He's going to beat me again when we get back."

"Stand up to him. Don't take it."

The boy looked up at James. "Easy for you to say."

"I assure you," James said, "I learned early that this place is a glorified gladiator ring with the guards as spectators."

The boy turned his head to look at the guards. "They don't stop it until I bleed."

"Malachi knows how to hurt without making you bleed."

"I know." The boy sighed. "Can you help me?"

James felt his heartstrings get pulled. The boy was asking to be his weakness.

After a long look around, focusing for a moment on Baba, he said, "I'll do what I can."

James knew the remote-viewing spell, but didn't dare use it in the prison, even in his cell. His cell had special wards that were just for his specific magic. Some things, like seeing auras, were natural for him, and no amount of wards or sigils could stop him from doing it if he concentrated.

He also paid close attention to the prison scuttlebutt. It seemed a long time before he heard about Malachi getting his ass served to him by a lanky little kid. He tried to gather details, but no one seemed to know, One second Malachi was going after the kid, and the next, the kid threw Malachi against the wall. It took three guards to pull the kid off.

James didn't see the boy for quite a while. Their release into the "courtyard" seemed to never coincide. Intentionally or not, he didn't know. Time passed strangely in this prison. He had lost track of days, months, years since he had been put in.

Eventually, he chose to forget about the boy and, the day he decided that, he went out into the courtyard for his normal exercise and saw him.

He had changed. No longer crouched in the corner, frightened and shaking, he stood against the wall, leaning back, his arms crossed. He seemed to observe the room, a young man watching everything with a cautious air. James checked his aura. Still dark, but more red and white streaks than he remembered. This meant that he was getting stronger, both in will and spirit.

As James approached, the boy stood straight and smiled. It was the first time James had seen him smile since the boy came in.

"You look good," said James. He wasn't sure, but boy had aged, grown taller. He was still skinny.

"You too," said the boy. "It's been a while."

"Certainly. I was about to give up hope of seeing you again."

"You said, the last time that I talked to you, that you would help me."

"Yes." James narrowed his eyes. What kind of favor was he going to be asked?

"I want you to teach me everything you know. And introduce me to Baba so she can do the same."

"Why? You can't use it."

"I want to know. I want to learn. The library only has books like *To Kill a Mockingbird* and *Stranger in a Strange Land.*"

James shrugged. "I suppose I could do that. But you would have to memorize it."

"I have a good memory."

"First, is it true that you beat Malachi?"

"Yes. He's left me alone since then. In fact, he wants me to join his group, but I'm not a Satanist."

"I understand. Most of us aren't."

Then the boy stepped in close and asked James, "Will you tell me what you're in for?"

James was the one who blinked this time. He stepped back, wary. "You don't need to know that."

"Is it that bad?"

"To the Rosicrucians, it is. To me, it's even worse."

"You feel remorse. They keep telling me that if I feel remorse and confess that they'll take that into consideration."

"That's just the thing, kid. I don't feel remorse." James crossed his arms. "Have you gone to the Confessor?"

"They keep bringing me to him, but I have nothing to confess," the boy said, as if he regurgitated the line often. He crouched down. "Show me what you know."

James glanced at the guards, then back at the boy's expectant face. "I'll teach you how to summon fire."

The boy called himself Grimaulkin. James introduced him to Baba, who introduced him to Malcolm, a forty-year old ex-Satanist who could teach him the black arts. Malcolm was a preachy type, though. James knew that Grimaulkin would have to sit through a lecture of how bad black magic was before actually getting the spell out of Malcolm.

James also introduced Grimaulkin to the weight lifters. Bierman, a big tough German ex-pat who got caught murdering his girlfriend as a sacrifice to "The Devil", gave the once-over to Grimaulkin.

"You do what we tell you," Bierman told him in no uncertain terms. "No complaining."

Grimaulkin nodded, and James knew that Bierman was going to be tough on the boy. But the boy needed toughness.

Bierman, for his part, introduced him to Rox, an ex-boxer with a chiseled square jaw that looked solid enough to break rocks. He also had a horrible temper. Once Grimaulkin expressed an interest in boxing, Rox seemed to calm down greatly.

Rox had no apparent reason to be in the prison. No one knew why he was in, and no one dared ask him because he would punch them out. Word had it that Grimaulkin was the only one who knew why Rox was in, and he wasn't telling anyone.

Throughout the entire time that James taught Grimaulkin spells, one of the guards kept watching carefully. James knew that the guard had a specific interest in Grimaulkin. But he didn't stop James from teaching him the remote-viewing spell, spells and sigils to summon angels, the calls and commands for angels and demons.

One afternoon, after Grimaulkin repeatedly drew in the dirt the correct sigil for Mahashel, an angel that bound the demon that caused disease, he asked James, "How can you summon an angel without being pure in heart and deed?"

James laughed. "You've been talking to the Jesuit, haven't you?"

"Well, yeah," he said. "You must have been pure in heart and deed."

"Maybe at one time."

"Don't you feel bad about what you did?"

James looked directly at Grimaulkin. This wasn't the first time he had brought this up. The other times were indirect. This time, he was totally straightforward.

"We discussed this." James stood up from his crouch. Yes, the guard was still watching them. "Do you feel bad about what you did?"

Grimaulkin rose, but his head was down. "No."

"Then you can understand."

"But you can fake it."

"You can't fake past the Confessors."

Grimaulkin looked up to see the guard watching them.

"We'll figure it out someday," Grimaulkin said quietly.

"Repeat the words," said James, to Grimaulkin as they walked around the courtyard.

"*Deus meus, ex toto corde poenitet me omnium meorum peccatorum …*" James nodded, listening to the lilt of the Latin words, the exact pitch, the exact cadence of the Spell of Penitence, a spell that would banish the angel Uriel to do work of redemption.

Funny, James thought, as he heard the words. *Funny that after this, I'm going to ask for my own redemption.*

"You have it," said James, as they completed one circuit of the courtyard. James stopped. Grimaulkin took one step and, after realizing James stopped, he also halted and turned around.

"That's it, kid."

"What do you mean, that's it?"

"That's the last spell that I know." James kicked at the dust of the concrete floor. "You've wrung it all out of me. Now I have nothing left."

Grimaulkin would have put his hands in his pockets, if he had any pockets in his uniform. Instead he brushed his hands on his thighs.

"What happens now?"

James gave him a wan smile. "If you'll excuse me, I have an appointment." He didn't touch Grimaulkin. It would show weakness, affection, something he didn't want the boy to know he had.

He walked over to the gate and said to the guard, "I need to see the Confessor."

James walked into the small alcove of the chapel and slipped into the confessional. To the man on the other side, of the grated window, he explained his remorse. He would no longer do what the Rosicrucians accused him of doing. He took responsibility.

He felt a giant weight slide off his shoulders.

He met Grimaulkin in the courtyard a couple of days later. He was lifting weights, and stopped when James entered. Grimaulkin looked much bigger than the little boy he had first met.

"I told the Confessor," James told him.

Grimaulkin patted James' shoulder. "They'll let you go now."

"Maybe, maybe not."

James started walking away from the weight area. Grimaulkin followed. When they got a short distance away, he turned to Grimaulkin.

"I set my wife and children on fire," James said. "Burning them alive."

Grimaulkin had heard so many stories from other witches and wizards, that he at least did not drop his jaw. His eyes widened instead. "Why?"

"As offerings to Baphomet." He looked Grimaulkin straight in the eye. "When I taught you the spells, I decided I don't need them anymore. I surrender myself to God's will and judgment."

"I won't see you again," Grimaulkin said.

James laughed. "I didn't teach you divination."

Then Grimaulkin did the worst thing he could have done: he hugged James.

James stiffened under the embrace, something that hadn't happened in years, and something he felt he didn't deserve.

The whistle blew.

James was released mere days later.

THE JAILER'S TALE

Why Ritter is so personal with Mike.

"Slither" by Velvet Revolver and
"Inside the Fire" by Disturbed

R ITTER STALKED THE CATWALK between the prison cells embedded into the walls. Three-inch-thick iron bars hung lengthwise and crosswise in front of each cell. Directly in front of the cell was empty air — a ten-story drop onto concrete. The catwalk stood six feet away from the front of the cell.

Ritter mentally counted the number of cells, and stopped before Number Six. A boy, young and thin, sat alone in the cell.

Ritter muttered the spell, and a plank of wood flowed out from the cell to the catwalk. Poles rose every foot, and a railing formed between the poles, as the bars from the cell flowed up to the ceiling on their own.

The boy stood up and walked to the doorway of the cell. "Come out, 150413."

The boy held onto the railing as he approached the catwalk.

When he reached it, the wood let go and fell toward the floor below — but never hit it, disappearing before it touched the ground.

"Where are you taking me?"

"To the Confessor."

"Why? I didn't do anything."

Ritter said nothing, giving the boy a gentle shove toward the end of the catwalk. The two guards at the end of the catwalk fell into place beside them, while Ritter walked behind the boy.

The boy glanced back at Ritter. "I swear, I'm not doing anything wrong. I'm meditating."

"Walk," ordered Ritter.

They left the cell area and continued through the prison, passing the visitor's area to the Confessors' offices.

Ritter heard through scuttlebutt that Prisoner 150413 called himself "Grimaulkin" in the yard. He looked up the word, and found it spelled without the "aw" sound. It meant an old female cat, and was the name the three witches of Macbeth called their cat.

Why would he choose the name of a cat?

He hoped the Confessor would get that out of him. He wasn't forthcoming since the fight a couple of days ago. Prisoner 150413 and another prisoner, yard-named Malachi, got into a sudden brawl that took six guards to pull apart. The boy was fierce—something unusual.

Yes, Prisoner 150413 was due for a visit to the Confessor.

Ritter stopped the boy by putting a hand on his elbow. The boy had learned to stop when touched by the guard.

"Here," Ritter said, knocking on the fourth door down the hallway.

"Enter," called a voice.

Ritter opened the door. He guided Prisoner 150413 into the office.

It was sparsely decorated, the walls painted industrial green, with no obvious artwork except a framed picture of a landscape on the desk. The man who sat at the desk looked in his early thirties. He wore a polo shirt and khakis with loafers and no socks. Ritter frowned at the lack of conservative dress — either the man was a hireling for the Rosicrucians, or he was new to the organization. He'd have to set him straight.

"Captain," said the man at the desk.

Ritter winced. He was never called by his title. "Confessor," he retorted.

"Hm, yes." He turned to Prisoner 150413. "Please, sit down. How would you like to be addressed?"

"Grimaulkin," said the boy.

"So noted in the file that Prisoner 150413 prefers to be known by the nickname 'Grimaulkin'." The Confessor looked up at Ritter.

"So noted," said Ritter. He didn't like the name, but he would have to use it in official correspondence now.

"Tell me why you're here, Grimaulkin."

"I didn't do anything," said the boy. "He told me I had to come here."

"What about the fight?"

"That?" Grimaulkin blushed. "A mistake, that's all."

"Explain it to me."

"I got a little excited."

"Let's start from the beginning."

Grimaulkin sighed, and sat back on the chair. Ritter calmly stood at parade rest, though he wanted Grimaulkin to come clean and stop beating around the bush. He could step in at any time to give the report, but it was time the boy took responsibility for his own actions.

"You went into the showers, and Malachi was there."

Grimaulkin sat up. "Fine. You're in my head, so you tell me."

"I'm not in your head. You're thinking loudly." The Confessor smiled. "So after Malachi approached you, you punched him. What did he say?"

"He didn't say anything."

"You punched him for no reason?"

"I punched him for lots of reasons. He's always been an ahhh, jerk."

"You can cuss if you feel the need."

Ritter raised an eyebrow. He knew now that the man was a psychologist or psychiatrist with some magical training — enough to skim the thoughts of prisoners without diving too deep. Or …

Ritter looked around the room, half-closing his eyes. He could see the runes and sigils embedded in the ceiling. The shrink had enough training to activate the runes to his benefit. That explained him being so open with Prisoner 15 — Grimaulkin.

Meanwhile, Grimaulkin was hedging his statements, which wasn't unusual in the prison population. The boy had been here only six months and had learned fast.

The Confessor released Grimaulkin without any useful information. Ritter knew something was different about the boy that would make him suddenly punch another prisoner. He only hoped it wasn't permanent.

Ritter slowly walked Grimaulkin back to his cell. Something was wrong, he could tell, and the Confessor didn't see it.

Maybe he should change to one of the main Confessors — the ones who can actually mind-read.

As he walked, Grimaulkin muttered to himself. Ritter couldn't catch any of the words, but the sing-song of them was a chant or a spell. The entire prison was warded against spells by the prisoners. Even if it was a spell, it would fizzle out before it got anywhere.

Ritter watched Grimaulkin go back into his cell. He was quiet, following orders as expected.

"Where'd you go?" asked the man in the cell next to Grimaulkin.

"Confessor."

"Again?"

Ritter didn't stick around to hear the rest of the conversation.

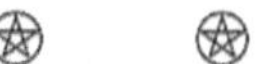

"Hey, Ritter," came the Pathfinder's voice in the locker room.

He turned to face the young blond mage. He smiled at him, reserving that smile for only a very few people.

"Aaron," Ritter said. "How's tracking?"

"Busy as usual. I miss having you at my back. What are you doing now?"

"Guard rotation here."

"You know you don't have to do that anymore."

"I know, but there's someone here."

"The boy mage."

Ritter was pole-axed by the statement. "How —"

"I could tell." Aaron pointed to his temple. "You were curious."

"The boy summoned Belial. Belial!"

"For the murder of eight people. Don't forget that."

"He's a prodigy."

Aaron raised an eyebrow at that. "Oh?"

"If we turn him to our side, he'll be a great benefit to our cause."

"I don't think he wants to banish demons. Did you ever find out why he summoned Belial?"

"He was being beaten up at school." Ritter slowly tilted his head. "Of course."

"Of course … what?"

"Why he went after Malachi. He was probably being beaten up by him, if not physically, then at least mentally."

"Do you need me to find out?" He grinned. "I have spells for that."

"That's truthspelling, and we're not allowed to do that once they're apprehended."

"I forget. You're by the book."

"If he tried to escape …"

"Or is thinking of escape?"

Ritter waved a hand. "Nah. Too much paperwork."

Aaron laughed and clapped a hand on Ritter's shoulder. "You know," he said, "I want to redo the runes on Prisoner 150413's cell. I think he's trying spells."

"We can do that without the paperwork."

"Mind helping me with that?"

"Right now?"

Ritter ducked into the locker and pulled out his guard uniform. "Might as well."

"Back again so soon?" asked Grimaulkin as Ritter summoned the catwalk to his cell.

Two guards and Aaron accompanied him this time.

"Step out here," Ritter commanded, when the iron bars flowed upward.

Grimaulkin came out, and Ritter put a pair of handcuffs on his wrists.

"What's this about?" Grimaulkin asked Ritter.

"Safety precautions," Ritter said, as Aaron walked across the plank to the cell.

Aaron whispered a spell, and he floated in the air to the ceiling.

"What are you doing?" Grimaulkin asked in a panic. "Stop!"

Ritter walked across the plank into Grimaulkin's cell.

Aaron redrew all the runes and sigils, while Grimaulkin stood outside, frowning. Ritter went through the items in his cell.

He found a notebook that had gibberish written in it. It contained Latin letters, but words that he didn't know. He could take it to a cryptographer and certainly find out what it said. He took the notebook.

Even if it contained spells, there was nothing Grimaulkin could do in the prison because of the wards. Why would he learn spells when he stayed in prison?

Ritter went through the cell meticulously, searching in all the typical hiding places:, such as under the mattress, pillow, testing out the walls for loose stones, the vent, even the ceiling. Aaron finished his work, and was sweating from the exertion.

"I think I got everything," he said.

Ritter nodded. He beckoned for Grimaulkin to return, and the guard gave him a little shove onto the narrow walkway.

Grimaulkin slowly crept his way across, not having any way to balance himself, with the railings on either side the only thing saving him from a ten-foot drop.

Ritter pulled Grimaulkin into the cell and undid his cuffs. Grimaulkin rubbed his wrists.

"What's all this about?"

"Just making sure you're not dealing in contraband," said Aaron.

"Ritter!" called the guard at the walkway, and he pointed to his body microphone. "You're wanted upstairs."

Ritter hissed, almost saying the word he was thinking: *Shit.*

The warden of the prison was in charge of three prisons around the world. Today he happened to be in New York.

When Ritter went "upstairs" to the main office, he came face to face not only with the warden, but with the head of the Rosicrucians — a mysterious man called Ezekiel.

Ritter removed his hat and stood at attention when he walked into the warden's office.

"Ease, Knight," said the warden, a well-built older man with gray hair and ice blue eyes.

Ritter, holding his hat, put his hands behind his back. "You wanted to see me, sir?"

"We both did, since we're here," said Ezekiel.

He was also older, but bald, with a wide gray mustache, and muddy brown eyes. His olive skin betrayed his Mediterranean roots.

"Yes, sir," said Ritter.

"Rumor says that you're interested in the youngest prisoner we've ever had."

"Yes, sir."

The two men looked at each other. "Professional, I hope?" asked Ezekiel.

"Sir?" Ritter blinked. What the hell were they thinking?

"The prisoner is homosexual," said the warden, "and might be attracted to you."

"Sir, it is entirely professional." Ritter tried hard to keep the cutting edge out of his voice.

To think, that they would think he would be interested in Prisoner 150413 in that way ...

"We need to convert the boy back to heterosexual leanings," continued the warden.

"You, Ritter, are not conductive to that," said Ezekiel. "Basically, you are relieved of guard duty. You will be exclusively out in the field."

"Yes, sir," Ritter stated.

The boy would be left to his own devices, and subject to conversion therapy. Ritter would have no say in the matter.

But he knew what that meant, and the boy would break. It would be bad for the boy.

Why should he care?

He vaguely heard the dismissal, but his mind was reeling. They would destroy his core beliefs. They would make him into something he wasn't.

He couldn't protect him. Or could he?

"What is it now?" demanded Grimaulkin as Ritter approached the cell.

He hadn't brought up the bars, but he did summon the walkway so that he could approach the cell.

"I have to go," Ritter said quietly as he stood outside of the cell.

Grimaulkin had to come closer. "Why?"

"Personal reasons. But I'll try and be back soon. I'm going to warn you, they're going to try conversion therapy on you."

"What's that?"

Ritter sighed. "You'll know when you see it. Just … remember, it's not you."

"I don't know what you mean, Captain."

Ritter shook his head. "It's complicated. Just be safe, okay? No more fights."

"I don't plan on any."

"I'll do what I can to come back and see you."

"Why do you care?"

Ritter started to turn around to leave, and then turned back.

"Because you're too young for this life, Grimaulkin."

THE PRODIGAL'S TALE

How the Gray Man became a Knight.

"What I've Done" by LINKIN PARK

OLIVER WAITHE RUSHED FROM ONE END OF THE STREET to the other. *Somebody stop the sirens*, he wanted to scream. *We know we're being bombed!*

The full moon illuminated not only the rubble in the street, but the planes overhead as well. He risked a glance up and could have sworn he saw the swastika on one of the planes. But that was impossible, unless they were flying *that* low.

Oliver tripped over some rocks, and he fell head-forward toward the cobblestones. His felt cap went flying off his head as he slammed his hands down on the stones to break his fall.

Someone grabbed him and hauled him up by the collar. "C'mon, laddie!"

He heard the whine of a bomb. Whoever had grabbed him yanked him under a stone archway. The bomb hit, at least a hundred meters away, but it sounded like it landed in front of him. Oliver ducked instinctively and would have run but the man who picked him up held him tight.

"We have to get below!" the man yelled at him, though it sounded muffled in Oliver's ears after the bomb had gone off so close to him.

The man pulled Oliver out from under the safety of the archway, and they dashed through the street to the tube's entranceway. They ran down the stairs, into the twilight recesses of the tunnel. Down here, everything sounded so distant, the *booms* mere *whumps* and shudders.

That's when Oliver noticed the priest's collar. *Oh, no,* he thought. He was going to get another lecture.

But the priest didn't seem to want to talk, leading Oliver further into the tube. Oliver thought he could see other people gathered in the dimness of the area, people who had small fires going. He could smell food over the dust of the constant bombing.

"Father Raymond," said one of the women, and then she looked at Oliver. "Found us a stray, didja?"

"It seems so. Feed the boy, if you would?"

"What about you?"

He waved a dismissive hand. "I am sustained by God."

"Until you collapse. Eat," she said, putting a newspaper-wrapped something in his hand. Oliver got a packet as well.

He smelled the corned beef before actually seeing it. Not a fan, but he hadn't eaten anything of substance in what seemed like days. He fell on it like a ravenous wolf.

Father Raymond spread his on crackers and ate slowly. "What's your name, boy?"

"Sliver," said Oliver, giving his street name.

"Sliver? That doesn't sound like a name a mother would give a son."

"It's a name I got," Oliver said, as he finished his little packet. His stomach growled for more, but there was nothing left.

However, Father Raymond handed over some crackers. "Fine, Sliver, but eat this slowly."

He nibbled on the crackers, and found himself calming in the priest's presence. The *whoomps* outside stopped, but no one moved from the tube.

"What do you do for a living, Sliver?"

I'm a thief, was his immediate answer. He said nothing.

"It's unsavory, whatever you do."

"I don't hurt anyone that don't deserve it."

"You're God's sword-arm," said Raymond with a smile. "I see."

Oliver blushed. When put in those words, it sounded so fake — like an excuse to rob and plunder the rich and give to the poor — namely, himself.

"Come walk with me," Raymond said.

They walked out of the firelight to the gloom of the station. He followed Raymond until they go to a bench. It was a little unusual to find a bench there, as it was between stops and located in the wall, cut out from the stone itself.

"Sit," Raymond said, sitting down.

Oliver had to jump up a bit to sit in the high seat. His feet dangled above the floor.

"The Rosicrucians, the Knights of the Rosy Cross, are looking for young men like you to help fill their ranks."

"Knights? On horseback?" He could barely ride a bicycle, never mind a horse.

Raymond chuckled. "Not unless you like that. No, Sliver, we're recruiting spies."

Oliver's eyes widened. Raymond chuckled.

"So you're intrigued?"

"Do I go to Germany, or —"

"Maybe. Do you know German?"

"No."

"French?"

"No."

"Then we'll teach you." Raymond turned and looked directly at Oliver. "Do you believe in God?"

"Yes." Oliver had his doubts sometimes, but if it meant his immortal soul, then yes, he did.

"Do you believe in angels, demons, or spirits?"

"Well …"

"Do you believe in magic?"

Oliver burst out laughing. "Of course not."

"Better get up, then," Raymond said, standing up from the bench.

Oliver did. The moment his feet touched the floor, he heard a low rumble, like rock sliding against rock. He watched in the gloom as the bench retreated into the wall and disappeared. He touched the area: it was smooth.

Father Raymond asked again, "Do you believe in magic?"

Oliver snapped his head up at Raymond. "Can you teach me that?"

"Do you want to be a full Knight?"

"If that's what I have to do."

Raymond laughed. "Let's see how you do with French, first."

Oliver didn't think he could learn French, but he surprised himself and Father Raymond by learning a local dialect of French from someone who had come from Vichy France. By the time he was ready to go to France, however, the Allies had already invaded.

During his training, the Rosicrucians found that Oliver did not have the gift of languages. His lower-class British accent came through no matter what he tried to learn. So, instead, they tried to teach him standard American English, so he would lose his accent.

Father Raymond grew old. Even with the help of the Rosicrucians and their magic, he aged quickly. His dark hair went gray prematurely. He was injured once during one of the last bombings in London and walked with a limp thereafter.

But he didn't lose his faculties, not even at the end, in 1962, when he went to sleep and didn't wake up.

At the time, Oliver was debating whether to join the Rosicrucians as a Knight. He got the call late in the evening at his apartment in Ohio, where he lived with three other men in the Rosicrucians. One was a Pathfinder, and two were healers. He was the only one not a member — and the only one who hadn't been trained in magic.

When he hung up the phone, the Pathfinder asked him what he was going to do.

"Sleep on it," Oliver said.

He prayed, something he hadn't done in a few years. "Tell me what to do," he asked God or whoever was listening. Then he slept.

He didn't remember the dream upon awakening, but he had a sense that Father Raymond had visited in his dream.

Oliver called the main office in Dayton. "I want to take the oath of a knight," he said.

"Please come by at noon."

Oliver wore his best clothes. His Pathfinder friend brought him to the office.

He entered the main office to see an older male receptionist. "Someone will be with you shortly, Oliver."

He'd never met the man before in his life. "You know me?"

"You have an appointment."

For a moment, Oliver thought he was in the presence of a mind-reader. He relaxed and sat on the leather couch, waiting until noon.

Right before noon, a side door opened and a man in jeans and a polo stepped out. "Oliver Waithe?"

Oliver stood up, realizing he was probably overdressed for the occasion.

"I'm Joseph Knight. Please, follow me."

Oliver got up and followed the man into the depths of the office. He went into a side office--a conference room, surrounded on three sides by windows.

A man stood with a sword in the corner. He smiled at Oliver. "Are you prepared to take the Oath?"

"Yes," Oliver said. The man lifted the Claymore blade onto the table, laying it flat.

"Place your hands on the blade and swear."

"Swear what?"

"Whatever is in your heart," said Joseph. "Every man's Oath is different."

He placed his hand on the blade. *Lord God, please accept me as your Knight.*

Oliver felt nothing. No grace, no sense of purity of purpose. He looked up at the two men, who frowned.

"You need to go on a quest," said the man who held the sword. "She's not accepting your Oath."

Joseph took the blade and handed it to the other man. "Do you truly want to be a knight? Is anyone forcing you into this?"

"A friend died recently."

"Mourn him, then come back."

Oliver put his hands in his pockets. God rejected him.

Well, the hell with Him, too.

He went back to his room, packed enough for an overnight, gathered his savings and flew back to London.

He didn't bother checking into the hostel that the Rosicrucians used, instead staying in a flea-infested hotel in London. It was the the mid-1960's, and London was the place to be for free love and new music.

A place for rebels.

Oliver didn't bother mourning Father Raymond. His funeral had passed, and Oliver didn't know where his grave was.

Oliver had spent his life since meeting Father Raymond with the Rosicrucians. He had worked with them, learned with them, and was ready to take the Oath to serve with them.

In the hotel, he kept bumping into a girl—or at least, he thought she was a girl—who wore leather and combat boots, cut her hair short and smoked cigarettes. She was alone most of the time.

One time he caught her sitting alone in the common room that passed for the hotel lobby. Her skirt was so small it looked like a sash, and she wore a cut-off vest buttoned strategically to cover her breasts.

Oliver summoned up the courage to approach. She was cute, even with the short hair.

"Hello," he said, slipping into his old accent.

She looked up at him. "Hello. I thought you were a square from the way you look. But you don't sound it."

He chuckled. "Looks can be deceiving. I'm Oliver."

"Marie."

Neither held out their hand for greeting.

"Waiting for someone?"

"My mates."

"Want company?"

Marie shrugged. Oliver took the lead and sat down.

Marie's "mates" never showed—if they existed at all. Marie explained to Oliver all about "The Scene".

Then they went upstairs and spent the night together in Oliver's room.

Oliver, though he was on the older side, fell into "the Scene" like a fish to water. For two weeks, he and Marie spent their time together, nearly inseparable. Marie took him on pub crawls, to concerts, parties, poetry slams, and more parties.

Then, it was over.

Oliver woke up one morning and Marie wasn't there. She wasn't in her room, either. The hotel clerk said she had checked out in the middle of the night. Oliver went out that evening to try and find her, but at every party, every concert, every pub, he was ostracized. He was too old. Too Square.

It was two a.m. on a Saturday night when he finally realized that he was no longer wanted. He wandered to the cemetery and found its gates open.

Oliver was in that type of mood, not to whistle past the graveyard, but to actually go inside it. He wandered into the dark shadows of the graves, deep into the cemetery, where even the starlight didn't shine.

He offhandedly looked for Father Raymond's grave, not knowing if this was where he was buried. But the gravestones were so old that he couldn't read the names, and it was too dark to even if he tried. He wandered down the paths, looking from side to side, looking for a freshly dug grave.

But this cemetery was far too old. No one had been buried here for years. He came out of the other end of the cemetery, almost bumping into two men standing just outside the gates. They were dressed from head to toe in leather.

"Are you ready?" one asked.

Oliver looked from one to the other. "Me?"

The speaker made a motion with his hand, and the ground erupted behind him. A coffin flew up out of the grave. It slammed into the fence, shattering, pouring out a skeleton that splattered against the fence. Bits of bone, dust and clothes landed on Oliver.

He screamed. The two men laughed, as Oliver stood, frozen.

"Do it again!" said the other man.

Oliver took a deep breath. "No," he said. "Don't desecrate the dead."

"What do you care, Knight?" said the first speaker.

The second man put his hands in the pockets of his leather jacket and rocked back. "He's a Knight? He doesn't have the eyes for it."

The first speaker got closer, right in Oliver's face, standing nose-to-nose with him. The man studied Oliver's eyes, flicking his gaze to above his head and back to his eyes.

"One way to find out," said the first man. Oliver heard the snick of a switchblade.

Oliver had been trained to knife fight before he was a teenager. Instead of backing off, he shoved the man's chest, as the man tried to stab him in the gut. Caught off balance, the man stumbled back, and Oliver closed the distance. He grabbed the man's wrist and twisted it backward.

The man grunted, dropping the knife, while his mate jumped onto Oliver's back. Oliver backed into the fence, and the man on his back screamed as the skeleton grabbed at them.

Oliver hadn't expected the skeleton to be alive. He jerked forward, pulling himself away from the screaming man and kicking forward, knocking out the knife-wielding man's legs from under him.

The second man kept screaming.

Oliver kicked the knife into the gutter. The first man looked up at Oliver.

"OKay, mate, you win."

Finally, the second man freed himself from the grasping skeleton and bolted across the empty street.

"Take care of this," Oliver ordered the first man.

"You take care of it, Knight." The man scrambled up and followed his mate across the street.

The skeleton's jaw hung open, its face pressed against the fence. The one arm that was still attached to the torso reached for Oliver through the fence. He wasn't a Knight. He had no idea what to do.

Oliver followed his instinct. He prayed.

"Dear Lord, in Jesus' name, be at peace. Rest the eternal rest of the dead, until Jesus summons you to rise again. Go back, return to your slumber."

The skeleton pressed itself against the fence so hard that its ribs snapped and fell to the ground.

"Please," he said, sounding desperate. "Please go back."

Then he heard the squeal of tires behind him. A black car stopped right next to him. Oliver knew without looking that it was the Rosicrucians.

The Pathfinder got out first. He looked Oliver over, but the Knight was the one who grabbed him, throwing him into the car.

"I didn't summon it!" Oliver cried out as the door slammed shut, encasing him in darkness.

Oliver looked out through the window to see the Knight and Pathfinder work to put the skeleton back in its grave. The Knight did the work of burying it while the Pathfinder came into the car.

"What's your name?" the Pathfinder demanded.

"Oliver Waithe. I was with the Rosicrucians until a few months ago. God rejected my Oath."

The Pathfinder waited until the Knight came back into the car.

"Take him to the office," he said. "He's one of us."

The Pathfinder kept a hand on Oliver's shoulder as he entered the office. No one was in the place this early in the morning.

They brought him into a room where swords hung on every wall. The Knight approached one and removed one from the wall, unsheathing it from its scabbard.

"Swear," the Knight ordered, holding the blade out, its tip resting on the arm of a chair.

Oliver put his hand on the blade. "I swear."

Then he felt it. A warm sense flowed over him—like hot water from a shower over his chilled body. It covered him and filled him with grace and power.

He was named Oliver Knight.

THE SQUIRE'S TALE

Chevalier means "knight" in French. He was never called that as a youth, but he chose to keep his father's name.

"Bulletproof" by Godsmack

CHRISTOPHER CHEVALIER DUG HIS FOOT INTO THE DIRT and raised the bat. The helmet didn't fit well on his head, as it was meant to be used by every batter on the team. He raised his head, even higher than usual, to keep his eye on the ball in the pitcher's hand. The pitcher nodded, then wound up. Chris's heart sped up. He saw the ball release and come at him.

Was it high enough? At the right speed? When … when … NOW!

He swung. He heard the crack of the bat. The ball aimed high up in the air. It would be an out, but he bolted for the base anyway. His helmet flew off his head as he turned to watch where the ball headed. He half-ran, half-jogged to the base, waiting to see if the outfielder would catch the ball.

He did —

And dropped it.

Chris poured on the speed and dove for the base.

"SAFE!"

The crowd roared. For him. Grinning, his friend Larry brought over his baseball cap as the applause faded and the next batter stepped up. He proceeded to hit the ball directly to the outfielder who wasn't going mess up twice in a row. Chris bolted back to first and got there in plenty of time, because the outfielder threw to the second baseman instead of the first.

It didn't matter. It was the third out, and the last play of the embarrassing game, with the Warriors losing to the Falcons four to six.

After shaking hands with his opponents, he looked for his mother. She wasn't in the stands. There would be no mistaking her Bohemian look among all these other fit and proper housewives. He gathered his gear and trudged heavily to the parking lot.

Chris saw his mother, her bright and curly red hair cascading down her yellow puffy shirt, her purple skirt flowing to her feet. She wore slippers—moccasins, really—and had her back to him. She was talking to a tall man in a black suit and dark sunglasses; he looked like he was in the Mafia or FBI.

Chris knew who the man was by the cut of his hair--thick and brown like his own.

"Dad!" He ran across the parking lot, tripped over his cleats, and fell face-first onto the asphalt.

Someone laughed, but the laugh was cut short as he saw his father come out from in front of his mother. Christopher never wanted to be on the receiving end of the kind of glare his father gave whoever laughed at him.

Larry bent down and helped him up. Chris's face burned, both from hitting the ground and the embarrassment. Chris' father nodded to Larry and brushed the stones from Chris' face.

"Are you all right?" asked his dad.

"Yeah."

"Then give me a hug."

Chris smiled and fell into his father's arms. After the hug, Chris turned to Larry, whose mother arrived.

"Larry, this is my dad."

Larry held out his hand. "Nice to meet you, Mr. Chevalier."

"Pleasure's mine, son."

His father's deep Virginia tones made Chris smile. People here in Braintree didn't know what to make of him. Some people needed him to repeat himself. When that happened, he would switch to his "official voice" or, as his mother called it, "The NPR Voice".

His father turned to Chris. "Ready to go home?"

"Yes."

His father picked up the gear and they went to the truck his mother drove. Always a trendsetter, she had bought an F150 when most people were buying Toyota Camrys or Honda Civics.

"How long are you going to be here this time, Dad?"

"Forever."

Chris was thrilled to pieces when his father said he wouldn't be leaving. He was the only child, supposedly for the reason that his parents hardly ever got together. But as time went on, he found out the real reason.

It wasn't soon after his arrival home that his mother took him aside to tell him that he was going to have a little brother or sister. Chris wasn't that excited. His mother prepared a special place in their bedroom while his father prepared to get another house or apartment.

During the summer, they searched for a place to live so Chris wouldn't feel as badly or be displaced too much at the start of school.

He found himself at Johnston Middle School the same month as his sister Ariana was born. They lived in a house off Route 5 — where the t raffic was atrocious from Route 195.

The traffic was the least of Chris's problems. The house … there was something strange about it. It made noise in the night. It creaked — trees rustled against windows, all kinds of strange and mysterious noises assaulted him at night.

Then there were the black shapes. Out of the corner of his eye, he could see dark shapes like dogs or small people run by. Chris would turn to look directly, but nothing was there.

Early one Saturday morning, he washed his face and looked up in the mirror.

A man's face, with ram horns on the top of his head, stared back at him.

He shouted, more surprised than afraid. When he looked behind him, nothing was there. Then he looked back at the mirror. The apparition was gone.

Was he going crazy?

He didn't know who to tell — if anyone.

His parents? Anyone?

He chalked it up to remnants of a dream and pinched himself to make sure he was awake. He felt the pain, so knew it wasn't a dream.

Then he walked downstairs to make himself breakfast and get ready to settle in for Saturday morning cartoons.

At school on Monday, he went to the school library to see if he could find out anything about the mysterious man with horns. A well-worn tome in the religion section showed him pictures of demons. One seemed to be the man in the mirror.

He was, according to the text, a satyr that the Church changed into a demon.

That led him down a rabbit hole about the Catholic Church. He wasn't brought up with religion. He did know the real meaning of Christmas and Easter, but he and his family never celebrated it that way. They gave gifts, celebrated with Santa and the Easter Bunny, respectively. This whole idea of demons and God was strange and frightening.

Was there a demon in his house? Or a satyr?

This library didn't have what he wanted: How to get rid of the demon/satyr.

As he closed yet another book he thought, *Maybe it was a one-time thing.*

Sunday morning, after looking up all the information on demons in the Johnston Public library on Saturday, he walked downstairs and passed the hallway mirror.

The demon stood behind him.

Chris bit back a scream. The demon grinned—yellow, pointy teeth in a dark maw. Chris turned around slowly, knowing he wouldn't see anything.

And, indeed, nothing was there.

His father came down the stairs right then, and Chris focused on him. *Should he say anything?*

"Everything okay?" asked his father.

"Yeah." Chris looked in the mirror. Just him and his dad. No man with horns.

"You should try out for a sport. Give us something to do on Saturdays."

"I want to be a cop."

"You have to chase people and be in good physical condition. It's a good idea to have a sport under your belt."

"I'll play baseball again."

His father rustled his hair. "We'll start practicing outside later if you want. There's a baseball diamond down the street."

Chris nodded, and smiled up at his dad, the man with the horns forgotten for the moment.

✹   ✹   ✹

"Chris, can you go to the bedroom and get the batteries out of the remote?"

Chris got up from the floor in front of the TV. Ariana was being fussy again. His mother was trying to calm her down. Nothing worked.

"How come?"

"Clock stopped again and we're out of batteries."

Chris went upstairs into his parents' bedroom. He walked over to the nightstand and saw the remote on the far nightstand. He picked it up, and saw a leather book beneath it. It was old, dark red leather, with a star embossed on it. He opened the book to the first page.

"Handbook"

The pages were thick and bumpy. He turned to the next page.

Written in beautiful script was the word "Knight" at the top of the page.

Next line: "Limited magic. Police force."

Police force?

"Chris!"

Ariana wailed from downstairs. Chris pulled out the batteries and ran back downstairs.

His mother stood there, Ariana on her hip, the baby screaming in her ear. "Chris, can you—"

Chris dashed into the kitchen, pulled down the clock. His mother followed him in with the squalling baby.

As he put the batteries in the clock, Ariana seemed to calm down finally. His exhausted mother plopped into his father's recliner, the baby on her chest.

"I'm gonna go upstairs," Chris said.

His mother nodded as Ariana seemed to fall asleep. He wanted to go read more of the book on the nightstand.

He ran upstairs and into his parents' bedroom. He beelined for the book, a fish on a line, and moved the empty remote to the side. He picked up the book. It was heavy and awkward.

He opened to the middle of the book, but nothing was written on those middle pages. Just the beginning.

After "Knight" came:

"Doctors"

"Healers & magic. Psychopomps.

"Knights: Heals wounds, physical & spiritual."

As soon as he read the phrase, the book flipped back to the "Knight" entry. Under "Police Force" was a new line:

"Doctors: Protect and get out of the way. Ask for assistance after civilians are saved."

After the "Doctors" page was:

"Pathfinders

"Guides, magicians. Seers. Second-line healers.

Under "Doctors": "Pathfinders: assistant healer. Magicians."

Under "Knights": "Pathfinders: Guides and possible assist. Typically partnered in most circumstances."

Then his mother screamed.

The paramedics seemed to give Chris' mother the once-over as they left the house. It seemed that Ariana had slipped out of his mother's arms and ended up on the floor. She didn't scream or cry out when she hit the floor. In fact, she was unresponsive when his mother woke up—which perpetrated the scream and phone call for an ambulance.

The look from the paramedic seemed to say, "Bad Mom," though Chris knew that wasn't true.

His father pulled into the driveway as the paramedics were packing the truck. His father jumped out of the car as soon as he parked it and ran up to his mother, who held a squirming Ariana.

"What happened?" he asked, looking at Mom, Ariana, and last at Chris.

"Bill," his mother began, then broke down and cried.

It bothered Chris to see his mother like this.

"Pat," said his father, embracing her. Chris saw the paramedics watching them. They judged. Chris looked back at them, with a burning fury growing inside him. His mother was not a bad mom. She panicked.

Ariana started up again and his father took her from his mother.

"Let's go inside," he said.

Immediately, Ariana quieted down and cooed.

His father seemed to always have a calming effect on Ariana. "I'll put her to bed," he said. "Go get yourself a cup of coffee."

His mother nodded and went into the kitchen. She didn't make coffee. She made something with fruit juice.

"Can I have some?" Chris asked.

His mom poured him an apple juice with ice. She sipped her juice and leaned on the counter, sighing, looking out the window.

Chris took his juice and went back to the living room. His father came downstairs, glanced at him and smiled, before going into the kitchen.

Dinner was going to be late.

Ariana was a horror to his mom. She refused to eat, sleep, or even be happy around her. His mother started to resent the child — at least, that's what Chris thought. His father fed Ariana her bottle, played with her, got her to smile and laugh.

His mother, not so much.

Chris, meanwhile, would sneak upstairs to read the heavy book. He learned about some club called "The Rosicrucians". They were a brotherhood, a knighthood, a police force against bad magicians.

How as his father involved with them?

He found an entry, "Banishment of demons".

Prescribe the Circle for banishment.

Chris knew what that meant from looking back in the book. He had to make a circle—which consisted of salt—and prescribe it by touching the edge and willing it to be for a specific reason. In this case, it was for banishment.

Call the Powers.

The Powers were whatever personal angels or guardians the Rosicrucian magician worked with.

Place the item in the center of the Circle.

Chris heard Ariana cry again. He wondered.

What if Ariana was possessed?

He looked again at the banishment instructions. He could do that. All he needed was some salt and … *angels?*

There were four Archangels according to the book. He supposed he should pick one. He decided on Rafael, because there was a Teenage Mutant Ninja Turtle by that name, and Teenage Mutant Ninja Turtles were cool.

Chris went back to the book, but the rest of the spell didn't want to reveal itself. He assumed that he needed to perform the spell to get the rest of it.

Ariana screamed again.

He nodded to himself.

Tonight.

Chris waited until the light went off in his parents' room. He heard his father moving, then, soon enough, no noise.

He slowly slunk his way to the door to his parents' room. He was apprehensive, not sure if it was safe to go in.

Chris glanced at Ariana's room. She was quiet for the moment but at any time, she would scream in the night, and force his parents to wake up. No, he had to swallow his fear. He thought of what Rafael would do.

He tried the door — unlocked. He slowly opened the door and padded barefoot across the carpeted room, silent as a ninja — or so he liked to think. In the dim light, Chris saw the remote sitting on top of the book.

He slowly moved the remote and picked up the book. He waited, but his father's snore made him feel relieved. Holding the book against his chest, Chris left the room and closed the door, the latch making a loud click. He held his breath. Nothing happened.

Chris went downstairs to the kitchen. He pulled down a cannister of iodized salt from the cabinet. He crept back upstairs, going into Ariana's room. He shut the door, looked around the floor in her room. The only clear spot was in the middle of the floor.

He poured out the salt into an oval-shaped area. Then he opened the book to the banishment page.

Call the Powers.

"Rafael," he whispered. "I choose you."

He pictured the *sai*-wielding turtle (adding wings) in his mind. He read the book.

Place the item in the center of the Circle.

He reached into the crib and slowly pulled Ariana out. She shook in her sleep. He placed her gently in the middle of the oval. The next two lines showed up in the book.

Pray, 'Lord, in your name banish this demon from hence

"... and bless this house," said a voice in front of him.

Chris jerked his head up to see the man with the horns. Black, crackling skin covered his entire body.

"G'head," said the man. "Say it."

"Lord, banish this demon from hence and —"

The door swung open and his father stood there with a sword as tall as Chris.

"What do you want, Flouros?" demanded his father.

He pointed at Ariana, who it seemed, sparkled.

"Bless the child," said the man with the horns.

"That'll be the day." His father raised the sword, point up. "Begone, damn creature. Begone from my sight."

He slowly tipped the blade down, until it pointed at Flouros' chest.

"Your father plans to kill me — kill us," said the horned man to Chris. "After me, it's you. Because he doesn't love you any more."

Chris looked up at his father.

"Don't listen to him, Chris."

"Who does he comfort? Not you. Your momma comforts you. You won't be a man."

"Stop it, Flouros."

"He comforts her —" He pointed again at Ariana, who definitely did sparkle. "Not you anymore."

His father glared at Flouros.

"Give me the girl and you will get your father back."

Chris blinked.

"Don't do it Chris. You're protecting her."

"Do you want to protect her? Why? She's in the way —"

"Chris, come out here." The sword didn't waver, and neither did his father's gaze on the creature. "Please."

"Now he begs." Flouros chuckled.

"Flouros, you cut too close."

"I speak the truth. Bring the child to me."

Chris looked at his father, who wasn't even looking at him, only at Flouros.

Was it true? Did his father love Ariana more than him?

Chris turned his gaze to Ariana. He knew that Flouros would do something horrible to her.

His father stepped into the room.

"Chris, get out. I don't want you to see this."

"You can't kill me, Knight. I live in your soul!"

Knight?

It all made sense now. The time away from home. The sword in his father's hand. The book on the floor. His father was a cop — a magical cop.

Chris walked over to his father and stood behind him.

Flouros *tsk*ed. "Bad choice, boy."

He tried to go after Ariana, but the Circle around her protected her. His father moved, stabbing forward, slamming the blade into Flouros' back. Instead of blood, light flowed out from the wound, glowing all around Flouros.

"I will feast on your soul when you die, Knight!"

"Get in line," his father said, pulling the sword upward through his chest, up past his head.

The light was so bright that Chris had to shield his eyes.

And then Flouros was gone.

His father panted, leaning on the sword. He turned to Chris. "Are you all right?"

Chris nodded. His father put his arm around Chris's shoulders and pulled him close.

"You weren't supposed to get the book until I was done with it," his father said. He separated himself from Chris and looked down at him, then placed his hands on Chris' shoulders. "I guess you're ready for it now."

"Is Ariana possessed?"

"No. She was probably sensitive to him. I'll have to ward this house." He smiled at Chris. "You did good, Chris."

He almost beamed. "Thanks, Dad."

"Let's put Ariana back in her crib and go to bed. I can ward your room before you go to sleep."

Chris watched his father use a pen and draw symbols on the threshold of Ariana's room, then Chris'.

"I'll paint them over tomorrow. This should do for tonight."

Chris thought he could feel the magic when he passed through the door.

"Try and get some sleep." His father held the book in the crook of his arm. "Tomorrow, we'll talk."

THE TALE OF THE UNICORN

"So what do you want in a man?"

Becky blushed as red as her sweater. Mike sat back in his chair at the coffee house and sipped his tea, using it to hide his grin.

Becky stared at her coffee. "He's a unicorn."

"Try me."

"He's got to be cute."

"A given."

"And funny. But not all the time. You know what I mean?"

"Appropriately funny and serious."

Becky nodded. "Long hair."

"Oh?"

"Deep voice."

Mike smiled. "You've thought a lot about this."

"I've had too many screw ups, Mikey."

Mike laughed. "What if I send the man to you?"

Becky looked horrified. "No, don't do that."

"It's not that hard."

"Let it happen naturally."

"I hate to see you get screwed over every time you go out with someone. Magic is to be used. Magic doesn't want to see you suffer."

Becky blew on her coffee. "God sends us suffering to learn lessons."

"God has a weird way of teaching you things. C'mon, work with me here."

Becky sipped her cooling coffee. "I know you want to help, Mikey."

"Especially after what I put you through. I want you happy."

"Let me think about it."

Mike reached across the table and patted Becky's hand. "That's a good first step."

After Mike left, Becky went to her car, her mind swimming. Could Mike find her the perfect mate? What if the guy Mike sent her was a psycho killer in disguise?

It's no worse than the losers you've gone out with the past couple of years, she thought.

She got in her car and drove back to her new apartment in Attleboro. She had graduated from the medical assistant class, and was trying to find a permanent job at a doctor's office. The job she was placed in after graduation was more secretarial, but it paid the bills. She wanted to continue her education, get a phlebotomist's license, and work in a hospital. She didn't want to be a nurse, but she wanted to have hands-on interaction with patients.

Becky parked on the street in front of her apartment. The porch was empty — it being close to winter — so she didn't have to say hello to her neighbors. She went around to the back door and went up the narrow hallway to her second-floor apartment.

It was a four-room apartment. She was happy with its size and location, and her neighbors were friendly and quiet. Her life was comfortable and boring.

Did I really need a man in my life?

Monday, and the office was in turmoil.

Doctor Stringer, the main physician on call, found himself late for his office appointments, which meant his patients were grumpy. Grumpy patients passed it onto the staff, who did their best to ease people's anger and frustration.

Most of the patients were on the older side, and probably had nothing better to do today, but they made it seem like their time was the most valuable in the world. Even Becky, who was known in the office as the most gentle and easy-going of the staff members, had to bite her tongue when a squat old man demanded that she either put him in a room right now or he would see another doctor.

He left, but called back to reschedule and didn't apologize.

At three o'clock, the office staff knew they would be there until well past six, so started to request volunteers of people to reschedule. Most did, disgusted as they were. When the last patient checked out at 7:20 p.m., everyone behind the desk breathed a sigh of relief.

The office manager came out and dropped into one of the chairs. "What a bad day."

The cleaning crew was already getting to their section, so the secretaries and medical assistants started getting their coats. Most of them had worked for almost twelve hours.

Becky drove to the nearest pizza place and ordered a chicken cutlet sub sandwich. As she waited, she watched people come in and out.

Would Mikey send a handsome man to me in a pizza parlor?

She laughed to herself. *Impossible.* Especially after the day she'd had.

"Number 45."

She got up, fumbling with her wallet.

"It's taken care of."

She tilted her head at the cook. "Who?"

The cook glanced to the door, and she turned to look, but no one was there.

"Thanks," Becky said, and picked up her sandwich.

She went outside and saw a man in a truck. He waved out the window to her, his hand holding a hand-rolled cigarette that smelled like cloves.

Becky approached the man. He turned from her and picked up something from the seat beside him. He held it out to her.

A red rose greeted her. She couldn't see the man clearly in the dim light of the truck.

"A rose for a diamond," he said.

She could only see that he had long blond hair. He waved the rose at her.

She took it. It had no thorns.

He started the truck, smiled at her, and pulled out of the parking spot, leaving her standing there. She put her nose in the rose. It smelled of cloves and roses, deep earth and high flowery light.

Becky debated on going back to the pizza parlor. Would she seem too eager if she did go back?

Finally, on Thursday, she couldn't take it any longer. She pulled into the pizza parlor and saw the truck. It had a Massachusetts license plate, and the driver's side window was open. The scent of cloves washed over her as she walked by it.

It was neat inside the cab, with the exception of a single rose on the passenger seat.

The door to the parlor opened, and the man from the truck stepped out. Of course he could see her looking in the truck, since the parlor had plate glass windows, and he had parked right in front of them. She backed away, but he came to her.

He was well-built, with broad shoulders and chest, and wore a black t-shirt with a pocket on the breast. His jeans were relaxed-fit, not too tight. He wore high-top sneakers.

"Hello," he said and smiled at her.

"Hi." She shifted from one foot to another.

"I have something for you."

She nodded to the truck. "A rose?"

"You beat me to it."

"I appreciate it."

He held out his hand. "My name's Dale."

"Becky."

She shook his hand firmly. His grip was gentle. Warm. She smelled the cloves, and she knew, right from that moment, that Mike had sent her the unicorn she always wanted.

THE ROGUE'S TALE

Thought it was the end of the reverend in Grimaulkin Tempted?
He really shouldn't have suffered a witch to live.

"Enemy" by Days of the New (including lyrics) and
"Unglued" by Stone Temple Pilots

R EVEREND RICHARD GREENE RAISED HIS HANDS TO THE SKY in benediction to his small flock before him. Five couples stood with King James Bibles in hand, all open to the same psalm, as they sang praises to God and the reverend who had done something to heal them or a member of their family. Three cancer cures, and other cures of mental illness, had greatly multiplied the group during the eight months he had been in Cincinnati.

He was well on his way to start a New Life Church. One of the couples was a lawyer, and she believed in him implicitly. She tithed thirty percent of her pay, which she could well afford, although her husband complained that they no longer had the extra funds for fun and pleasure.

Reverend Greene had learned his lesson after the year and a half away from the Waters of Life: *Do not flaunt the money.*

New Life rented a modest storefront for their services in an up-and-coming section of the city, close enough to the upper crust, yet not too far from the rougher section of town, either.

Reverend Greene lowered his arms and felt the power rush from him to his people — the ones who believed, who trusted him. He knew which ones they were. Two of them were paying lip service, already thinking he was a cult, and trying to figure out how to get out of the group without disturbing their daughter who had been cured of a tumor in her lungs just a month before.

He concentrated on them. As he did, the doors burst open.

A man stood in the doorway, holding a white wooden staff. A young man. A young man Greene thought he had taken care of.

"You," Greene said.

"There you are, you son of a bitch."

The young man pointed the staff at Greene. Purple light flew from its tip, slamming into the podium before Greene. The podium exploded, sending shards of wood every which way.

"You tried to kill me," the young man cried, advancing into the room.

Greene ducked to the back of the room, following along the rear of the stage, keeping the members between him and the advancing blond man.

The blond slammed the end of the staff into the floor and took a deep breath. Greene had reached the end of the stage. Four feet of empty space separated him from the back door.

Someone tackled the young man, sending him flying against the edge of the stage. Greene dove the four feet and tried the door. Locked.

Oh, how stupid!

The young witch rolled out from under the other man, and using the staff as a bat, he clobbered the man in the ribs. The wood held. The witch flipped the staff and aimed its tip again at Greene.

"I take your magic away!"

Greene didn't know where to run. The young man threw the staff. Greene ran sideways, but the tip of the staff hit him in the leg, sending him to the floor.

He felt blood leak out of him.

No, not blood.

Greene looked down at the broken staff at his feet. A puddle of golden light lay between its broken bits.

The young witch was taken down again, this time by three other people. They held him until the doors burst open again and the police came.

But, by then, it was too late.

The young witch laughed as they took him away.

THE TALE OF
THE TWO RINGS

Mike tries to be romantic.

"*Ain't Too Proud to Beg*" by The Temptations (including lyrics)

M IKE OPENED THE DOOR TO THE JEWELER'S. He looked
around first, making sure he wasn't being followed. He
ducked into the place.

It was empty, except for a balding man in a suit standing
behind the counter. Mike nodded once and said, "Hello."

"Hello, sir. How can I help you?"

"I'm looking for an Italian gold wedding ring set."

"For yourself?"

"Yes."

The bald man smiled. "And the lucky lady?"

"No."

The smile might have slipped just a little. "It's a surprise,
then?"

"He's not a lady."

The smile faded.

Mike crossed his arms.

"Does this mean you don't sell to gay people?"

"My boss would kill me." He motioned to the wall. A framed picture of the Virgin Mary was there with a dollar bill stuck in the lower part of its frame.

"What about you?"

"I don't like the idea."

"You know, we're legal to get married now."

He brought his lips together tightly. "I know that."

"So you mean to tell me you'll go against the law?"

"The law doesn't say anything about selling wedding rings to people like you."

Mike tightened his crossed arms. "People like me."

"It says you can get married. It doesn't say I have to provide a service for it. That's still in the courts."

Mike knew he was right. He also knew that he wouldn't get a set of rings by going up and down Federal Hill, where the Italian and Catholic jewelers were located.

He sighed, relaxed his arms. "Help a guy out. Where can I find someone who'd sell me a set?"

"Try Providence Place?"

Mike frowned. "I need custom work on it."

"They do engravings."

"It's more than just an engraving." Mike looked up at him. "I need someone who loves to work with the metal, not have it punched out by a machine. It's special symbols."

The bald man looked back at the Virgin Mary. "If my boss finds out …"

"I won't tell anyone except my husband."

The bald man winced, not liking the word. "Okay, what's your size?"

"Nine."

"His?"

"Six."

He sighed, pulled out two rows of wedding bands. Mike picked the plainest, but thickest, one for both of them. He tucked a hand in the pocket of his denim jacket and pulled out a piece of yellowed paper.

"This is what I want engraved on the inside of both rings."

The bald man picked up the paper, scowling. Mike took it from him and turned it over. The man grabbed a pen and drew an arrow on the top of the slip of paper to show which way to hold it.

"What is this?"

"Enochian. The language of the angels."

"Right."

"Don't mess it up."

"Give me a week."

"A week? Can't you do it now?"

"I don't have anyone to watch the store. And if the boss comes in while I'm out back, I could get in trouble."

"Show me how to do it and I'll go do it myself," Mike said, disgusted.

"No. And no one in this town would let you."

Mike looked at the bands, then the paper in the man's hand. "Don't mess it up. I'm serious."

Mike left, and the bald man folded the rings into the paper.

"Language of the angels." He looked at the Virgin.

Mike left the jeweler's, his plans all in disarray. He had planned to propose to Scott that very night, to offer him the rings, and they would go to the town clerk the next day to make it official.

Mike walked into the apartment he and Scott shared. The roses he bought in the morning were still in the vase on the kitchen table. Mike sat down next to the roses and sighed.

It didn't take long until Scott returned home. Mike summoned some Chicken Marsala from the Italian place a few blocks away. Scott saw the dinner laid out for him as he walked in the door. He knew Mike couldn't cook.

"Where did you get it from this time?" asked Scott as he sat across from Mike.

"Trattora's."

"I hope you tipped the driver?"

Mike waved his head back and forth.

"Mike. We talked about you using that cornucopia spell before."

"I was in a rush. I'll go pay for it tomorrow."

"After you see me off at the airport."

"The airport?"

He speared a piece of chicken. "Conference in London. Two weeks."

"But, but …"

Scott smiled gently. "You forgot?"

Mike had forgotten, in the dizzying plans he made for the next week.

"It's … It's … You can't."

"I told you last month. I'm on six panels and a keynote speaker, babe. Why are you panicking?"

"I had something in mind. Plans. An idea."

"It'll have to wait," Scott said. "If it's Tantric, you'll just have to wait for the next planetary hour."

Mike hunched his shoulders.

Scott rose and came up behind him. "C'mon. Let's practice upstairs."

Mike traveled home via taxi from the airport. The apartment was silent, cold and empty.

Two weeks!

He'd lose his mind. First, the rings. He didn't know how long the magic would stay with them once he charged them with his specific spell — a spell that he only trusted one man with. Second, how could he get the ring to Scott?

Mike passed the jeweler's almost every day for a week, holding himself back from going in to check on the results of the rings. Finally, on the very same day of the week of his original visit, if not the hour, Mike walked into the jewelry store.

The bald man was not at the counter, but another man in a suit stood there. Younger, probably a couple of years older than Mike, with olive skin and dark, chiseled features. Mike smiled at him: now this was more his type.

"Hello," Mike said. "You have a pair of engraved gold rings for me."

"Let me see," said the man, his voice with a tinge of an accent Mike couldn't place.

The man pulled open a drawer and rummaged around. He pulled out a couple of boxes, opened them, and set them on the counter. There were engagement rings, wedding rings, silver and gold and white gold. Most had diamonds; some were plain. Mike picked up one box and checked the engraving inside the ring.

"This one," he said, holding up the box.

The man looked at it and frowned. "Two men's rings?"

Mike closed the box and tucked it in his pocket. "Times, they are a-changin'. How much?"

"Did Mr. Falici say it was all right?"

"Sure. How much?"

He charged for each ring, and for each letter of the engraving. Mike almost wanted to call out highway robbery, but he handed over the gold Amex card and closed his eyes, as if waiting for the hit to come. As he signed the slip and looked at the final total, he almost blanched. But he had the rings.

Mike left the store and jumped into the waiting taxi.

"Take me to the nearest travel agent." He forked over a twenty-dollar bill. "And wait there."

"You got it, mister," said the driver, pulling out into traffic.

Mike patted his inside pocket. He would put the magic into it when he put it on his husband's hand.

Mike flew on planes before and never liked them. He didn't like packing, didn't like the TSA, didn't like the helplessness he felt when being in a plane and letting someone else do the flying.

He talked his taxi driver into bringing him to Logan Airport in Boston, giving him a hundred-dollar tip for the trip up and back. The plane was leaving in two hours, and it took an hour for him to get to the airport. He didn't have to wait in line for the check-in. He had summoned his passport from home into the back of the car as it was barreling up Interstate 93.

Mike got to the TSA, saying a spell for speed. Half an hour to go before boarding. He was cutting it really close.

He took out the box with the rings and put it in the bin. The TSA held it in the x-ray machine a little too long.

Two men came over to him, one standing at the bin with his rings. "Is this yours?"

"Yes," Mike said. Twenty-five minutes.

"Mind opening it?"

Mike opened the box to show them the rings.

"What's underneath?"

Mike tilted his head. "Felt? I just got this from the jewelry shop."

"Take them out."

"I … I can't."

Both men's eyes went wide.

"It's complicated."

"Come with us."

"My plane is leaving in twenty minutes!"

"Without you. Put your shoes on and come with us."

"Goddammit, I don't have time for this."

He slammed shut the box, made a motion with his hand, and disappeared from their view.

"The hell!"

"Where'd he go?"

Mike slipped his shoes back on and gripped the box tightly as he dashed between people, avoiding touching them. However, he disturbed the air around them; some people stopped short as if nothing was there.

When he had a clear lane ahead of him, Mike sprinted to the gate, catching it just as the last few people were boarding. He released the spell and stood before the doors.

They beeped him through, and he didn't take a deep breath until he was buckled in his seat and the plane started taxiing away from the doors.

Mike landed in Heathrow in the dark. He couldn't sleep, not with the turbulence or being in the middle seat. Once released from the back of the plane, he summoned the "can't see me" spell just in case. Then he calmly walked to the front and right past the police officer that stood at the doorway, glancing at a phone and then up as people walked by.

Taxis lined up at the circular drive of the airport. He climbed into a taxi.

"No bags, mate?"

"Nope, just me."

"Where ya goin'?"

"Earl's Court."

"Ibis?"

"ILEC?"

"Ibis London, Earl's Court. Gotcha mate."

According to the travel agency, that was the only conference going on for two weeks straight. He asked the travel agent what it was for: "Diversity in the West and East." That kind of thing was right up Scott's alley, as they spent some time in Tokyo and could understand how the Japanese accepted homosexuals more readily than most other Eastern cultures.

Mike and the cabbie didn't talk much. Mike tried to think of what to do or say to Scott as he patted the box in his pocket. Should he just show up at his hotel room and present him with the rings right there? Or summon roses to fall on him on stage and propose to him there?

"Are you married?"

"Yeah," the cabbie responded.

"How did you propose to your wife?"

He chuckled. "Brought her out on the Thames where she couldn't escape."

"How did that work out?"

"We're still married; got two kids."

"So the key is to bring her someplace where she can't run away from you."

"That's how I would handle it."

Mike nodded, the plan forming in his mind.

Ibis was a series of buildings, including a conference center and a hotel. He went to the hotel first. Even at four a.m., the lobby was still busy.

Mike found his way to the front desk. He picked up a program for the conference and asked, "Are there any rooms left?"

The clerk looked at him as if he was crazy. But he turned to look it up anyway. "We have a suite available for two nights."

"I'll take it," he said, and presented the credit card.

It went through, and he was given a key card.

"Room 2014, sir."

As soon as Mike stepped into the room, he locked the door and went to the bedroom, stretching out on the bed.

"Just a nap," he said, and closed his eyes.

He heard Scott's ring tone on his phone after what seemed like only moments later. Mike fumbled in his pocket, pulling out the phone.

"You're sleeping?" asked Scott, after Mike mumbled a hello.

"Just a nap."

He glanced at the clock on the side of the bed. *Twelve thirty.* Lights squeezed through the blinds, so it was only the afternoon.

"Sorry I woke you up."

Mike pulled out the convention's program and scanned it, looking for Scott's name. "Don't you have a panel or something?"

"In between talks. I'm giving my keynote address in a half hour."

Mike sat up. "You're not nervous, are you?"

"Of course I'm nervous." Scott laughed. "Why would I call you in the middle of the morning?"

"You'll do fine. You always do."

"Thanks. I guess I'd better go get ready for it."

Mike found his name and the time. He was going to talk about Western versus Eastern homosexuality history. In half an hour.

"I love you," Mike said. "Break a leg."

"Love you, too. I'll try."

Mike hung up and went to the bathroom. After washing his hands quickly, he bolted out the door, patting the box.

He knew the speech Scott was going to give. He'd heard him practice it enough times. He knew there was a part in the speech about marriage: a throw-away line that marriage was a contract in some cases, so why couldn't it be the same thing in a same-sex marriage?

Mike dashed down the hallway, and waited, bouncing and swaying in anticipation of the elevator. One finally arrived, and Mike wondered whether he should have just run down the stairs. He jumped out of the elevator as soon as the doors opened.

He wove between crowds of people to the conference center. There weren't too many people in the room that he could see, so he picked a spot in the middle of the seating area. It started to fill up and, by the time the lights went down, it was almost full.

Scott stepped out with a wireless microphone clipped to his suit's lapel. Mike realized he was underdressed for what he was about to do.

"Hi, everybody. Thank you for coming."

Mike felt his heart swell with pride as Scott welcomed the people in, put them at ease with a joke, and went into his speech. Mike moved from his seat, slowly inching his way forward, toward the stage.

When Scott started into the facts about contracts and marriage, Mike stood up in the aisle at the front row. Scott had his back to him for a moment, and said to the audience, "Why can't there be—"

He saw Mike and stopped short.

Mike grinned, stepped toward the stage.

"Ladies and gentlemen," said Scott, "Meet my boyfriend, Mike."

There was some applause, and Mike climbed onto the stage. Scott looked up at Mike, and then watched as Mike dropped to one knee, pulling the box out of his jacket pocket.

The crowd cheered.

Mike opened the box.

"Will you marry me?" he asked. His voice projected through the room, which had gone silent with expectation.

Scott smiled, took a deep breath and replied, "Of course I'll marry you."

Mike took out Scott's ring, and placed it on his ring finger. Suddenly, a purple flame burst around Scott that cleansed him and made the audience gasp. When the flame died down, Mike handed the box to Scott.

Scott took the remaining ring and put it on Mike's finger. This time Mike turned into green fire, and he felt the love of his life seeping through him, into his very bones.

Then, Mike kissed Scott onstage. Mike didn't hear the cheering crowd, his ears filled only with the soft noises of his happy fiancé.

THE FAMILY'S TALE

I might be a technomancer.

"Where's the nearest bar?"

"I didn't HEAR what you said," the voice of the Mercedes told me.

Scott shook his head, grinning. "It doesn't work that way."

"WHERE'S THE NEAREST BAR?" I demanded.

"Please say the NUMBER you wish to call."

"Cancel," said Scott. "Stop confusing the truck, Mike."

"It's not a truck. It's a station wagon."

"SUV."

"A tall station wagon."

"Are you complaining about the vehicle I bought?"

"No. It's got heated seats."

Scott chuckled. "And a heated steering wheel."

I rolled my eyes and settled back in the leather seat.

"I called Evie to tell her we were coming. My father's supposed to be there."

"I thought he was in a nursing home?"

"They're bringing him home for the Thanksgiving holiday."

"So it's Dom's family, your father, and us. How many people?"

"Twenty-one, she said."

"Does she have room?"

"They're mostly kids."

"That's a lot of people, though."

"She has a big house."

"We have a bigger one. Want to do it next year?"

"Hell no!" I said.

The GPS chimed, "Bear RIGHT ... Connecticut Route 2 West ... Norwich/Hartford."

As he turned the wheel slightly, I could see the tungsten ring he wore on his left hand, exactly like the one on my own left hand. I smiled, knowing this would piss off my father. It was going to be an interesting Thanksgiving.

We decided to go to Connecticut on the Tuesday before Thanksgiving, even though we lived just across the state border in Scituate. It would take us three hours to get to Norwood. We wanted to spend some time with Evie, Dom, and my two nieces, Charlotte and Ashley. We hadn't seen them since our wedding in 2015.

When we pulled up to their house, I could hear dogs barking. It made me think of Rufus, who had died just after they moved out of the apartment into their first house. After that, they'd gotten a boxer and then a lab-shepherd mix. If Evie had her way, she would have come home with an entire shelter of dogs.

This was their second house. After Evie got a better job in the Connecticut school system, Dom became an editor at the *Hartford Currant*. Things fell into place for them, which I was happy for.

They had the room for a menagerie of animals, if they wanted. They had six acres of land in the back, and a quarter acre of lawn in the front. The split-level ranch house, although smaller than ours, had three bedrooms on the second floor, an open floor plan in the living room, and a huge kitchen. We parked the car in front of the house, on the street.

I walked over to the side of the house, which was fenced in. I could see the dogs on the other side. When they saw me, they rushed at the fence.

The sliding glass door opened, and a tall and lanky girl came out.

"Uncle Mikey!"

She bent down and patted her thighs, calling to the dogs, "Rusty! Grey! Come here."

The dogs reluctantly went to her.

I opened the fence lock, and Scott and I stepped inside. The dogs came up to us to inspect us.

"Hi, Charlotte," I said.

"Hi. Hi, Uncle Scott."

She had Evie's build, but Dom's Mediterranean dark looks, with long raven-black hair flowing down her back almost to her waist.

I gave her a hug and a kiss on the cheek; Scott did the same.

"Your mom home?" I asked.

"Yeah. She's cleaning."

"So that's why you're downstairs."

Charlotte shrugged. "Yeah, you know how she is when get gets to cleaning."

"You're not driving yet?" asked Scott.

"I need to get a car, first," she said. "Mom and Dad won't let me get a car until I get a job. Want to come inside?"

"Sure."

She let the dogs in first, then we followed her inside.

"Mom!" Charlotte yelled up the stairs. "Mom, Uncle Mikey and Scott are here!"

"Be right down!" Evie called back.

"We can always go up," Scott said to me.

"And step into her newly-cleaned area?" I asked in mock horror. "You'd inflict the wrath of the Gods on you."

Scott smiled and leaned on the kitchen island. Charlotte drank a Coke from the can.

"Got any diet?" I asked.

"Yep, just for you and Scott."

She ducked in the fridge and took out two Diet Cokes. She handed them to Scott and me. I heard people come down the stairs.

The first person I saw was a girl, about fifteen, with a short, spiked haircut. She wore a flannel shirt, jeans, and men's slippers. She stopped at the bottom step.

"Ashley?" I asked.

When I'd seen her at our wedding, she was in a light blue puffy dress, with lace and chiffon. She'd had long hair like her sister.

"Just Ash," she said, biting her lip.

I walked up to her. Evie stood behind her.

"Ash," I said, and looked her up and down. I knew what she was going for.

She looked down. Embarrassed, I think. I hugged her.

She exhaled. "You're not mad?"

"Why should I be mad?" I held her at arm's length. "This is very brave of you. It took me eighteen years to admit I was gay to my parents."

"I'm not gay," she said.

"You're trans," said Scott.

Ash nodded.

"Oh," I said.

Evie put a hand on Ash's shoulder and guided him to the side.

Scott smiled, and then came over and gave Ash a hug also. "You're kind of cute."

Ash blushed bright red.

I walked over to the counter to retrieve my Diet Coke.

Evie hugged me from behind. "I'm so glad you decided to come."

I leaned my head into her shoulder. "Wouldn't miss it."

"You missed last year."

"We were in Japan for six months. Scott's modeling career really took off there."

"They're mystified by red hair," he said.

Evie poured herself some lemonade. "What are you doing with your life, Mikey?"

"Doing the normal paranormal research and fighting the forces of evil. Nothing big."

Before she could ask me what that meant, the sliding glass door opened and Dom walked in.

"Hey, Mikey, Scott."

"Hey," Scott and I said.

I smiled as I understood that the Fates had stepped in so I wouldn't have to explain what I meant to Evie.

Dom absently pet the dogs. "That your Mercedes out there?"

"Yes," said Scott.

"Nice SUV. I'm jealous."

Dom gave each of us a hug. He kissed Charlotte and nodded to Ash. Ash nodded back.

"Staying for dinner?"

"We wouldn't want to put you out," I said.

"We'll put another pair of steaks on the grill."

"Grilling in November?"

"Do you see any snow on the ground?"

"No ..."

"Then it's grilling weather!" Dom gave Evie a kiss. "Going to change. I'll be right down to start dinner."

Evie smiled as he left. She looked like she was still in love with him. That was sweet to see. I hoped Scott and I would be like that.

Well, we had been together for over sixteen years. It looked promising.

Evie took out two steaks and put them in the microwave to defrost. "They're ribeyes. Do you mind?"

"Do I mind?" I asked. "They're steaks!"

"Don't you eat steak?"

I thumbed at Scott. "Model, here."

Evie stopped the microwave. "I might have some veggie patties in the free—"

Scott waved his hand. "It's okay. I'll run a little more on the treadmill tonight."

"We don't have a treadmill," said Evie.

Scott and I looked at each other. "We were going to a hotel in —" I said.

"Nonsense! You can sleep in one of the kids' rooms."

"Mom!" yelled Charlotte.

"They can sleep in my room," said Ash. "I have a full-sized bed."

"We won't put you out," I said firmly.

"We're going to have twenty-one people in a few days. You won't be in the way."

"I want to sleep on the couch," said Ash. "I can watch the good TV all night."

The "good TV" was a half-movie-screen-sized curved-screen television that took up almost the entire wall. If I watched TV, I could understand why he'd want to do that.

"Works for me," I said.

"Okay," said Scott, shrugging.

"We'll get the bags."

Magicians don't drink, but models do sometimes. We adults were sitting outside where the weather was chilly, but not freezing. Dom had a firepit burning. Evie and Scott both had some wine, Dom drank something amber with ice, and I had a bottled water.

"So when did Ashley decide she was a boy?" I asked, the question burning in my mind since I saw her.

"About six months ago," Evie said.

"It might be a phase," said Dom, swirling the amber liquid in his glass. "I treat her like I was treated. You know ... tough, 'Hey, bro', that kind of thing. I don't think she likes it that I don't hug her any more."

Scott looked into his wine glass.

"It might not be a phase," I said. "I was twelve when I knew."

"I was fourteen," said Scott.

Dom sipped his liquid. "Sorry. I didn't mean to insult you."

Evie put a hand on Dom's arm. "This is all new to us."

"You seem to be accepting it better than a lot of parents I've heard about," Scott said.

"What would you do?" asked Dom.

"I wouldn't deny her — him — from exploring," I said. "I ended up in prison for it and hating Dad."

"Do you still hate Dad?" Evie asked.

I didn't say anything, drinking to avoid answering the question. They stared at me, not wanting to let me get away with not answering.

Scott saved me. "You haven't seen him in years. He might have missed you."

"You don't know my father well, do you?"

"Your father is like my father was. But he still left me all his money."

"Because you're the only child."

"He could have left it to my cousins."

I could see that. "My father doesn't love me."

Evie looked horrified. "Mikey, that's not true."

"He loved Phil. He put everything into Phil. You know what Mom told me once? I was a mistake."

"Mikey, she had Alzheimer's. She probably didn't know what she was saying."

"Or she was telling me the truth for once."

Evie sighed.

"Let's talk about something other than how our parents suck," Dom said. "Are you a model, too?"

"No." I laughed. "I work for the Rosicrucians."

"The people who put you in prison?"

"I'm a magician for them. Sometime Knight, though I haven't taken the vows. I work with the Rhode Island State Police and other police in the northeast when they get weird cases."

"Are there a lot of those?"

"You'd be surprised."

"Must keep you busy," said Evie.

"Mostly around Halloween and some full moons. The serious ones are during the New Moons because they have a clue as to what they're doing." I probably could have gone on and on about my work, but they looked confused and tired at the same time.

Dom yawned, and that was the cue for us. He doused the fire.

⊛   ⊛   ⊛

When I woke up in a strange bed, I did what I normally did. I searched for the protective runes I automatically put up the night before. I looked over the side of the bed. The paper with the sigils on them had not been disturbed. I bent over, gathered them up, and placed them under the pillow.

Scott stirred next to me. "Is it safe?" he asked.

"Yes," I said.

I had learned to be overprotective to the point of paranoia. I knew this place was not a hotel. The house seemed to be too new to be haunted, and none of the kids were conjurers that I knew of, so no destructive spirits were in the vicinity. However, I had gone to too many places that were beautiful on the outside, but had a dark heart.

The bathroom was right next to the room, and I heard the shower going. It was sunrise, about the usual time we woke up.

"Want to go for a run?" Scott asked, always conscious of his exercise regimen.

"We can do that."

We arrived downstairs to find the morning chaos of kids getting ready for school, adults getting ready for work.

Evie gave me her house key. "I'll be a little late. I have some last-minute things to get at the market."

"Do you want an amulet to get you through the line faster?" I asked.

"You can do that?"

"It'll take me a few minutes."

"Can you do something like that for traffic?" asked Dom.

I wasn't sure if he was joking, but I went along with it anyway. "I'll make something more permanent for your car and send it to you."

As I drew the rune for speed confined by "harm none" and efficiency, Ash watched over my shoulder.

"That's so cool," he said.

I finished the drawing.

"It's on fire," he said.

I turned to look at him. "You can see that?"

"Can't you?" He looked at his mother, who seemed confused.

I put a hand on my hip. "Not everyone can see magic."

"That's magic?"

"That's how my magic manifests. Purple fire, right?"

"Yeah. You can't see it?" he asked his mother.

"I don't see anything but the mark on the paper."

I folded it up into a triangle and handed it to Evie. "The fire should be out, now," I said, watching Ash.

He nodded.

I put my hand on his shoulder. "We need to talk."

"Is there something wrong with me?"

I squeezed his shoulder and gave him my best smile. "Nothing's wrong with you," I said. "Nothing at all."

"When you get home from school, we can talk."

Ash grabbed her backpack and followed his sister outside to catch the bus.

"What was all that about?" asked Evie.

"He's got the makings of a magician."

Evie and Dom looked at each other. "I think you should talk to us first," said Dom.

"No reason why I can't talk to him first, to let him know what he could do. It's not like I'm going to test him."

"What does testing involve?"

"I wouldn't do any testing without your permission, Dom. He's still a minor."

"Which is why you should talk to us, first."

"Dom," said Evie. "We're going to be late."

Dom grabbed his briefcase and turned to the door. "Remember that he's a minor, Mike."

I gave them a few minutes, as Scott filled the water bottles. "Thinking of taking an apprentice, again?"

"Maybe," I said. The last one didn't quite work out. I was exonerated, but it was a close call.

We went running down the quiet side streets. Scott had a GPS on his phone, connected to his watch, so we didn't get too lost. We went out for about two hours at a leisurely pace, so we weren't out of breath when we got home.

Scott and I decided to go out for breakfast, so we found a little hole-in-the-wall joint that served some of the best home fries I'd ever had. Then I asked Scott if he would mind going to New Haven.

He knew why. He knew the way there — without the GPS.

Marjorie Lynn LeBonte
June 1, 1945 – July 3, 2008
Thomas James LeBonte
May 17, 1942 –

"Hi, Mom," I said.

Not to the tombstone, not to the body in the grave, not to the soul that didn't haunt the place. Maybe I said it to my heart.

Cancer felled her, but I took her. I remember that Evie couldn't stop crying, seeing my mother suffer, while my father kept refusing to take out the life-sustaining machinery. My father prolonged her suffering; I could see it. She lay in the hospital bed, her mind elsewhere, her soul tugging at the cord that connected to her body, wanting to be free.

I could talk to spirits, only with aid. I don't think my father would appreciate me to showing up with a Ouija board or drawing a conjuring circle in the middle of the hospital room in order to talk to my mother's spirit.

I walked into the hospital room alone. I had a scythe with me, just a small one, commonly called a _boline_. I saw the cord, silver and glittering, connected to her root *chakra*. With one swish of the *boline*, I severed the silver cord.

Her soul looked directly at me, shocked. That was microseconds before the machines beeped like crazy. I tucked the *boline* in my pocket as an avalanche of people ran into the room. They performed what they called "superhuman methods" to try and bring her back. That was, of course, my father's directive because he refused to authorize a "Do Not Resuscitate" order.

That shocked look is what causes me, sometimes, to wonder if what I did was what she wanted. Her soul never returned to me to admonish me that it was my fault; she never haunted me or anyone that I knew. She never came to her own funeral, either. But I wondered what that look was about.

I set the bouquet of roses on the tombstone, because that was what you did in scenes like this. Although she wasn't here and, while it was an empty gesture, it was expected.

"So, I get to see Dad tomorrow. Want me to say 'hello' to him for you? No? I don't blame you. He put you through hell for his own selfish reasons."

I squatted down and touched the dirt. Nope, she was nowhere nearby. It had been nine years, after all.

"I'm happily married now, Mom. No grandkids, like you predicted. I don't like little kids, anyway. I like them around Charlotte's age. High school. You can talk to them. Little kids, you can't hold a conversation with them." I smiled. "I'm not a motherly type, sorry."

I had asked her soul if she was angry with me, but got no answer. so I didn't bother with that question any more. I looked for a sign: a bird, a breeze, the sun disappearing behind clouds. Nothing. She was gone. Long gone.

I sighed, and then turned and picked my way along the graves back to the car. Scott waited, his nose in his phone, probably checking his email.

As I approached, he looked up at me. "Still empty?"

I nodded.

"That's a good thing, isn't it? She's really passed on."

"She's gone to her afterlife. She's with the angels."

I'd never see her again. Now I had to deal with my degenerating father.

We got back to the house just before the kids. They were on break now.

It was unseasonably warm, so we sat outside with the dogs in the back yard. Rusty was a sucker for a good game of fetch, while Grey would chase after Rusty. However, Grey always came back with the stick.

I rolled around on the lawn with the dogs, while Scott laughed at my antics. I loved dogs and animals more than most people. We didn't have pets because of our constant traveling, so any chance I got to spend with animals was heaven to me.

Ash and Charlotte caught me on the ground, tackled by Rusty. Grey ran to Charlotte and leapt on her. Charlotte jumped back, so the dog grazed her shirt, its claw catching it and tearing it.

"Okay, okay, guys," I called to the dogs, "Time to calm down. The adults are in the room."

Ash chuckled, while Charlotte stormed into the house to change her shirt. Grey followed her.

I got up, dusting dirt and grass bits off my clothes. Ash hung around outside. I could tell he wanted to talk.

"So," I said, going up to him. "Magic."

"Yeah," he said, looking down. "Um, do I have to do what you do?"

"What do you mean?"

"Mom told me you had to take medicine."

"At first I did, because it was overwhelming. But I learned how to work with what I could see and hear with what I could do and what was around me."

He looked up, confused.

"In other words," said Scott, "he got used to it."

I asked Ash, "Have you tried any magic?"

"Um, no."

"Want to?"

Ash both blushed and shuffled his feet.

"I can teach you."

"I don't think Dad wants me to."

"Probably not. He knows what I went through, but I had other things happen to me — things that may not happen to you."

"Like the prison?"

I sighed. It was part of the family history, and Evie must have told the kids why I disappeared for five years.

"Like the prison," I replied. "But I can keep you out of prison. Teach you the right way."

"Can I, like, think about it?"

"Of course you can. You have my number, right?"

Ash nodded.

"Just let me know. In the meantime, look up stuff on meditation."

"Meditation? That's so boring."

"Not if you do it right."

Scott gathered our lemonade glasses. "There's a lot of good meditation apps. You should try them."

"Sure," said Ash.

I doubted he would, though. We went into the house.

The temperature dipped and it was too cold for an outdoor campfire this night, which was good, because I wanted to be well-rested for my father and Dom's family the next day.

If I thought yesterday was chaos, Thanksgiving Day was sheer pandemonium.

It started at 9:30 in the morning, when Dom's father and newest girlfriend showed up. Ten years Dom's father's junior, she had a plastered-on clown face and smelled strongly of old roses. She even brought her own apron and immediately went to work in the kitchen.

Dom left at ten to go pick up my father from the nursing home. He left Scott and I with instructions on how to set up the tables for the adults and kids, and where the chairs and tablecloths and fine china were. Then people started showing up.

Kids. Too many kids. Too many *loud* kids. Everyone had their own phone or tablet and the TV was blaring. People bled into the bedrooms upstairs. Outside was freezing cold; the dogs had been put away in the garage. There was no escape.

By noon, I already had a pounding headache. Dom hadn't come back with my father yet.

Then Evie called to me over the din. "Mikey, can you go help Dom with Dad? He's in the driveway."

I threw on a coat and went outside, my heart pounding. I hadn't seen my dad in five years, by my own choice. I didn't invite him to the wedding because I knew he wouldn't have approved. What was I going to see?

Dom was standing on the passenger side, the door open. He saw me and I could see him breathe a sigh of relief. As I approached, I could see a man, bald, leaning forward in the seat, with his hands firmly on the dash.

"He's not very lucid today," said Dom as I came around the car. "It took them a half an hour to get his coat on."

I saw the man in the car. Still tall, but he was now mostly bones. He gripped the dash for dear life, not wanting to get out of the car.

"Dad," I said. "Dad, it's me."

"Phil?" he asked, looking up at me and blinking.

"No, Mike."

"Who's Mike?"

My stomach dropped. He didn't know me. He knew Phil, my brother that had died — that I had killed … years ago. I could do one of two things: argue with him, or go along with him.

"Yeah, I'm Phil," I said. I didn't sound excited about it, but if it got him out of the car, I would play along with it.

"Phil," he almost wailed, dragging the name out.

Then he started to sob. Dom shifted his weight from foot to foot as he held the handles of the wheelchair.

I sighed. I had seen the same thing happen with my mother. However, where I had patience with her, I didn't have any with him.

"You have to get out of the car, Dad."

He suddenly stopped crying, as if a switch had been pulled. He blinked up at me.

"Come on, Dad. Out."

I took his arm and tugged him. He swung his legs out of the car. I lifted him out of the car, turning his body so he could drop into the wheelchair Dom held still for me. I put his feet in the stirrups.

"Where are you taking me?" he asked.

"To see Evie."

"Where's Evie?"

"In the house."

Dom got him through the gate to the back of the house. We guided him into the house, where it was hot and loud. People finally realized that the big dinner could start now that the man of the house was back. Dom got his coat off, kissed his wife seconds before Evie kissed Dad on the cheek.

"Hi, Daddy."

"Evie?"

She brightened, and her eyes turned shiny. "Yes, Daddy."

"Where's Margie?"

"She's not here today," Evie told him. "You know Mike."

"That's Phil. I don't know any Mike."

Evie looked up at me, concerned.

I waved my hand. "Let it go, Evie."

I didn't bother introducing Scott, even though a lot of people said hello to my father. He wouldn't remember them.

Scott took me aside. "Are you okay?"

"I'm fine."

We all settled in to eat off the fine china using the fancy silverware. Evie and the kids set up the sides on the adults table and the kids table. Then came the turkey, which Dom proudly carried to its special spot on the adult's table.

Then he lifted his glass of champagne. Everyone else did as well.

"Let us give thanks, oh Lord, for the bounty here. For our family and friends. Let us have another year of good health and all be back next year."

"Cheers!" I said, and touched my glass to Scott's.

Dom's family said something in Italian, doing the same thing. Then Dom started cutting the turkey. He served my father first.

Evie cut up the turkey, asked Dad what he wanted. He told her. A moment of lucidity, I thought. Maybe this wouldn't be so bad.

All the food was great, because my sister is just that good of a cook. I was happy that we were here as a married couple. I was happy to see Evie happy, even though my father was scowling.

Then, suddenly, he threw a biscuit at Dom's brother. It skipped across his plate, into the gravy, and splattered on his shirt.

"What the hell!" Dom's brother jumped up and glared at my father.

My father glared right back.

"*Hold!*" I yelled, and time stopped.

Scott stood up. He was immune to my magic. I had the spell for that engraved in his ring.

"Your father's going to try to tip the table."

I squeezed behind Evie to my father at the corner of the table and moved the wheelchair back about a foot.

"What was that all about?" I asked.

"Probably got overwhelmed."

I went around the kitchen island, into the living room, and shut off the unattended TV while I was at it.

"So he takes a temper tantrum?"

"Or attention-seeking. The next thing he's going to do is comment about how the food is awful."

He was the diviner, not me.

"What should we do?"

"I would remove him entirely from the situation. He's like a four-year-old."

I went back and got the wheelchair, and moved it to the living area, parked him in front of the couch in case he would try and get up, he would fall face-first into it.

"*Resume!*"

Dom's brother opened his mouth to yell something at the empty space where my father had been.

I stood next to my father. He lifted his hands to flip the table over that was no longer there.

He turned to his left, where Evie had been sitting, and said, "This turkey is dry." Then he looked to the right to see only me. "What? Where's the table?"

"Act your age or you won't get any dessert," I said. "Apologize for throwing the bread."

"I didn't do anything." He crossed his arms and pouted.

"You're not going to let your age be an excuse."

Dom's brother wiped at his shirt — he was still steaming.

Scott muttered a spell, and the stain disappeared. We let him think that he wiped it away.

"Forget it," said Dom's brother, and sat down.

"Not hungry anyway," my father muttered.

"Suit yourself," I said, and went back to my place at the table.

"Mikey," Evie said when I sat down, "He should eat something."

"Feed him later when there's not so many people around."

Dinner then passed without further incident. No one noticed the TV was off.

It was quiet in the garage with Scott and the dogs. Dom had just left with my father, who ate nothing, no matter how Evie tried to feed him.

Ash came in, stepping around the car and water bowl for the dogs.

"A lot of people are gone now, Uncle Mikey."

"Came here to fetch me?" I asked, sitting on one of the lawn chairs we'd taken down from the wall.

"Kinda. You did something, didn't you? With Grandpa?"

"I moved him so he wouldn't hurt anyone."

"How?"

"I stopped time."

Ash's eyes went wide. "You can do that?"

"Yep."

"Oh, wow!"

"That's very advanced," I said, trying not to sound high-and-mighty. "Takes years to learn."

"Is that what you do, make sure nobody gets hurt?"

"Yes. I try to protect people or stop the bad guys."

Ash leaned against the car, petting Rusty. "How long does it take to learn that?"

"I'm still learning every day."

"I was thinking about it, you know? I think I want to try."

I stood up.

"Then I accept you as my apprentice."

Ash looked at my outstretched hand. He grinned, reached out and shook it firmly.

# THE APPRENTICE'S TALE

I read Beguiling Voices *by J. Dark and wondered what would Mike do in a similar circumstance. Here's my homage.*

"*Gasoline*" by Seether

I DIDN'T LIKE HANDLING THREE THOUSAND POUNDS OF METAL going seventy miles an hour down a road with other people behind the wheel of three thousand pounds of metal going even faster down that road. So I had Ash drive the Mercedes north to New Hampshire. We headed up Interstate 95 to investigate "something strange" — at least that's what the police dispatcher told me.

Ash had his driver's permit, because I still didn't have a license. Scott was supposed to teach him, but he was on a shoot in Tokyo. Although I had competition with DeLuna — and other witchy members in New England — nobody could beat my rates. That's because my husband was a model and I mooched off his money. But I kept the man very happy.

Ash was seventeen, and should be in school today, but I needed him to drive me the hundred or so miles north. Even though he wasn't supposed to cross state lines with the permit, I could probably spell my way out of any traffic stop. Scott would be upset if we got the Mercedes impounded.

"In one quarter mile, take the exit right," the Mercedes said to us through the speakers.

"Damn computers. I swear to God, they're going to take over the world."

"It's okay, Uncle. They're only as smart as we program them to be."

I grumbled, not happy with that answer. But then, Ash had more electronics in his front pocket than I could understand. Hell, I couldn't even set the alarm clock.

Ash took the next exit and followed the SUV's commands until we came to a small parking lot across from the city hall. The police station sat next door. Ash looked expectantly at me as he set the car in Park.

"Well, come on. You're my apprentice for a reason."

He nearly jumped out of the seat after he unbuckled the seatbelt. I smiled. I knew he would be happy to help.

I opened the door to the police station and let him in first. Habit, I guess. He opened the following door and let me in. I got to the dispatcher, a woman behind a wall of thick chicken-wire-filled glass.

"Can I help you?" she asked.

"I'm here to see Detective Mackenzie."

"One moment."

I wondered briefly if he was going to be a butch or a fem. Imagine my surprise when a woman came out and introduced herself as Mackenzie. Taller than Ash by a good half-foot, she wore a short bob of a haircut and wire-rimmed glasses. She had dark circles under her eyes and didn't seem to bother with makeup. She took my hand in a firm grip.

"Please come with me, Mr. LeBonte."

I followed her deep into the bowels of the police station, finally ending up in an interrogation room. She fetched an extra chair for Ash after I introduced him.

"So," I said, leaning my elbows on the table. "What seems to be the issue that needs my attention?"

Mackenzie didn't waste any time. "We have reason to believe that there is a cult operating in the city limits."

"That's not good. What kind of cult?"

"A devil worshiping cult."

"Of course. What I meant to say is what are they doing to give you the idea that they're a cult?"

"We rescued a girl, seven years old. She told us that they sacrifice babies and drink their blood."

"Did you do a welfare check?"

"We can't find them."

"And the girl isn't forthcoming?"

"She doesn't know, either."

"You sure she's not making up stories to get her parents into trouble?"

Mackenzie frowned. "We did think that. But then we found out that her parents had disappeared."

"Not that I don't want to work with you, but this sounds like something for the FBI."

"Mr. LeBonte, there's something strange going on up there and none of our guys want anything to do with it. The FBI won't go in without a warrant, and we can't go by the word of a seven-year-old girl."

I watched her closely. Something about this was personal. Although we sat in the station, in the interrogation room, this was something beyond the usual purview of the police. Detective Mackenzie had made this her crusade.

I cared where the money came from. So I asked her, "Is this personal?"

"For the entire department," she answered, not skipping a beat.

I sat back in the chair and risked a glance at Ash. He was doing his best to look disinterested, but his eyes were glassy with unshed tears. This bothered him to his very core and, for that reason, I pressed on.

"Can I speak to the girl?"

"No."

I knew that was going to happen. "Transcript? Video?"

"Yes, I can provide you with that."

"I'd like to see it before taking the case, if that's all right."

Mackenzie got up. "It's a two-hour long interrogation."

"We've got all day."

"I'll bring in the AV." She got up. "Coffee?"

I turned to Ash. "Coke?"

He nodded.

"Two Cokes, if you have them?"

"Sure."

We got our Cokes and a TV was wheeled in, with an extension cord that trailed out of the interrogation room. For two hours, we sat in the uncomfortable chairs and watched a cute brown-haired girl, clutching a woolen blanket like it was a lifeline, talk in a straight-up monotone about debaucheries and sacrifices of babies. Toward the end, the interrogator asked if she was abused, describing in detail about inappropriate touching. The girl was forthcoming. It made my blood boil.

At the end, I shut off the TV. Mackenzie didn't come in immediately.

I turned to Ash. "What do you think?"

"I think you should take it."

"I don't know. You'll be losing a few days of school."

He gave me an "Are you kidding?" look.

When Mackenzie came back, I asked, "Can I please have whatever files you might have collected on this case?"

"I'll talk to the IT department to get you cleared to look at them."

Computers. Dammit.

They had to contact Scituate police to do a background check on us. Of course, we had to wait until the next day, which meant we needed to stay overnight somewhere nearby.

Thankfully, it was off-season, so rates at the hotels were cheap. The bad news was that only the big hotels were open; none of the cute little bread-and-breakfasts.

I pulled out the expense account credit card and started racking up the airline points for Scott. We had only brought enough clothes for an overnight stay, but Kittery Outlet stores were just a few minutes up the road. Literally.

Scott called. It was early morning in Tokyo where he was.

"How's the tour?" I asked him.

"Great. They're treating me like a king. What are you up to?"

"I have a case."

"With Scituate?"

"No, Portsmouth."

"There's a Portsmouth in Rhode Island?"

I laughed. "New Hampshire."

"How did you get there?"

"Ash drove me."

"Mike. Ash has a permit."

"Yeah, I know."

"If you get stopped …"

"We won't get stopped. We're working for the cops."

He sighed. "Please be careful. This is Ash we're talking about. Your sister will kill you if anything happens to him."

Ash looked up at me from the bed next to mine. I smiled at him, but answered Scott.

"I'll be careful, I promise."

I hung up after giving Scott kisses over the line.

"You two are so cute," Ash said.

"He's the love of my life. What can I say? You'll find one."

"I'm not interested," he said. "Not right now." He looked down at his shirt, his chest. He frowned.

His body betrayed him. Ash had discussed transitioning with his parents, letting Scott and me know that he had decided that he would wait until he was eighteen and make his own decision. In the meantime, he bound his breasts tightly to his chest so that he wouldn't seem too feminine.

I got up and put my arm around his shoulders. "Let's worry about getting you where you need to be before Scott starts playing matchmaker."

He laughed. I squeezed his shoulders and headed to the bathroom.

I woke Ash early the next morning. He took a shower to wake up even more while I gathered our things. We went directly to the police station.

Detective Mackenzie wasn't there. The dispatcher, however, let us in. We stood in the doorway until a dark-skinned man in shirtsleeves and khakis came over to us.

"You LeBonte?"

"Yes," I said.

He thumbed at Ash. "Who's that?"

"My apprentice."

"You're cleared," he said to me. "She's not."

"*He,*" I corrected.

"Ashley Marcello. She's a minor."

"He's —"

Ash put his hand on my arm. "It's okay, Uncle. I'll wait out here."

He turned and left by the dispatcher's door, waiting outside in the hallway, his head down.

Was he crying?

"Come with me, LeBonte," said the man, and led me through to a computer terminal. He handed me a yellow square of sticky paper that had "Lebonte" at the top and "Kandi3$" underneath.

I deduced them to be my login and password. Hey, I might not be any good with computers, but I can at least type with two fingers and use a mouse.

I entered the information and one folder came up titled "689484". I clicked it open and found assorted image files were scattered throughout it. I clicked through them one by one.

They were scanned-in police reports: observations by the officers, pictures of the little girl with her face blurred out, pictures of where she was found. There was a list of places that they thought the compound was located, but there were no pictures, just descriptions of open landmarks.

Then I found pictures of the little girl's parents' apartment: abandoned, but full of items as if they had just up and left on an outing. The apartment was neat, the refrigerator and freezer full, and nothing really looked out of place … except for a picture of an empty closet.

Why an empty closet?

I sat back, staring at the picture. If I had the actual picture in hand, I could probably see what I wanted to see: the edges of a portal. Instead, all I had was an hypothesis.

I took down the names of the officers who had either found the girl or went into the apartment, and the apartment's address. Then I went to get Ash.

He was sitting quietly in the waiting room, texting, Tweeting, Facebooking — I have no idea what. I stopped at the dispatcher first.

"Is Officer Hector Gonzales available?"

"I can call him."

"Can you have him meet us at this address?" I wrote out the address on her sticky pad.

"All right," said the dispatcher, and immediately contacted him.

Meanwhile, I grabbed Ash. "Ash, we've got a dimensional portal. I think. I need your help."

He stood up, slipping his phone in his pocket. "Sure."

As we walked out, I explained, "I think there's a dimensional portal in this house, but I can't see it in the picture. I want you to try and see it."

"In the picture?"

"No. At the apartment."

We got inside the Mercedes and I told the GPS the address. Ash followed its directions to a side-by-side condominium. The address I had memorized was 142B, so we approached the left-hand side door.

I peered into the windows, which had no curtains on them. "It's been cleaned out," I said. "I guess it's for rent."

"We can call the landlord —"

But I already was heading around the back. Ash followed.

The back entrance was a sliding glass door. I stared at it with my arms crossed, wondering what spell to use to get us inside, when Ash peered around the corner of the house. "Uncle, police."

"Good," I said.

Officer Gonzales was handsome, even though he was bald and not usually my type. But I had a thing for uniforms, even way back.

"You looking for me?" he asked.

"Yes. Can we go in?"

"It's not a crime scene anymore."

"I think there's something still inside there that hasn't been cleaned out. Something magical."

He raised an eyebrow. "I don't know about that."

I smiled at him. "Most people don't. But my assistant here, he can see magic. I just need to get in there."

"We can call the landlord," said Gonzales.

"I don't think I have time for that."

"Can you get in?"

"Sure," I said.

"I'll call the landlord, tell him we're going in."

As he turned from me to talk into his shoulder microphone, I walked over to the sliding glass door. I put my hand over the upper lock, and willed it open. I heard the click as it unlocked.

When I pulled the door handle, however, it only moved about an inch. A piece of wood blocked the slider on the floor from the inside. All I had to do was lift the wood out of the way.

"Ash, wanna try something?"

He came over to me.

"See that white piece of wood? You need to move it. Remember the teleportation spell I taught you?"

"But don't I have to touch it?"

"You're going to try it without touching it. I know you can do it."

Ash smiled. I knew he could do this. He closed his eyes and bent down to put his hands on the glass. The officer stood silent and watched. It was like he didn't want to say anything to break the moment.

Ash said the spell out loud, articulating it in the right places, and the piece of wood disappeared. Ash moved his hands to the side of the deck, and the piece of wood reappeared from his hands, falling to the wood on the deck.

"Holy shit," the officer breathed.

Ash grinned. I clapped him on the back.

"Nice job."

I let Ash push open the sliding door. The officer stepped forward, a hand on his gun.

"I'll go in first."

We followed him. "I just want to go to check out the closets."

Gonzales nodded and we walked to a closet on the first floor. I had Ash peer inside. He shook his head.

We went upstairs to the other three bedrooms; there were closets in each. It wasn't until the master bedroom where Ash opened one and then jerked back as if shocked by something inside.

Gonzales came over and opened the door. "What?" he asked, looking inside the closet. "I don't see anything."

I opened the closet door wide. I couldn't see it full on, but if I looked out of the corner of my eye, I could see a red oval about the size of a page of paper on the opposite wall.

"What do you see?" I asked Ash.

"It's red and black and takes up the whole wall back there. It's like swirling …"

I smiled and put my arm around his shoulders. "So glad I brought you along."

"You're not going through it, are you?"

"Of course I am."

"I don't think that's a good idea," said Gonzales.

Ash bit his lip.

I stepped into the closet. I turned to Ash. He shook his head.

"I can't see it," I said to Ash. "You have to guide me through."

Both the officer and Ash didn't agree with my reckless curiosity.

"I'll protect you," I said.

Ash turned his eyes to the officer. Ash then sighed, and stepped forward into the closet. He took two steps ahead of me, and held his right hand out in front of him. I watched as his hand, then arm, then body, passed through the wall. He held his left hand out to me.

I took his hand. Even though I saw a wall, my body passed through it, like it passed through a lake. I shook myself, feeling like I had some residue on me, but I didn't.

I found myself in a windswept, snowy forest. Coming from fall into winter was unexpected, and we weren't dressed for it. Behind us we saw the oval, tucked between two trees.

"Oh, wow," Ash said.

That's how I felt, but I knew we would be too cold to feel anything soon. I debated going in further against going back and getting more winter clothing. A little voice said backup would be nice too.

Backup. Bah.

"Let's go look around," I said. "We won't go far."

"They'll see that we came through here," said Ash, looking at the snow on the ground.

If I covered the tracks, we wouldn't find our way back. If we let our tracks be seen, we could be followed.

That was a chance I'd have to take. Getting back was more important than being discovered.

We walked through the woods, maybe twenty or thirty yards, before we came face to face with a wire fence, topped with barbed wire. I peered through the fence and counted six buildings: five arranged in what looked like the points of a pentagram, and one building in the middle. Guard posts dotted its perimeter every fifty yards or so.

"They've been here a long time," I said. "Look at the buildings."

"What are we going to do?" Ash asked me.

"You're coming with us." The voice was not Ash's.

I turned around to face three men with guns pointed right at us.

I could probably have used magic to get us out of the situation; I could probably take out all three. But there was Ash to contend with. He didn't know enough offensive magic yet.

Part of me, however, was curious as to what was inside the buildings, and whether or not I could save the people inside—if that was what was in the buildings.

Yet, there was no way I could save them all.

Backup would be good.

I raised my hands in surrender, but muttered a spell. A bright light came out of my hands, blinding the three men and Ash. I grabbed Ash and started running.

I tripped over something in the woods and fell, but Ash grabbed me and pulled me to my feet. I heard the gunshots behind us, and knew we would be in trouble if we stopped.

We dove through the red oval and slammed into the closed closet door. I turned over, ready to throw a fireball at whoever — or whatever — might come through the oval. But nothing did.

That's when I realized the door was closed and Officer Gonzales was gone. We had left it open when we went through.

I pushed open the door. Outside, it was now dark.

I could hear voices from downstairs, but I couldn't understand what they were saying.

How long had we been in that other dimension?

Ash went pale. "There's someone —"

I nodded, and we left the master bedroom. Just as we got to the top of the stairs, I saw a man coming up it. He stopped when he saw us.

"Who —"

I smiled. "Just stopping in. Nice place you have here. Excuse us."

I started down the stairs. The man backed up, with a couple right behind him.

"You're the landlord, right?"

"Yes …"

"I'm with the police. We might be coming back."

"But they told me it was all right to rent."

I looked at the couple. "It's haunted."

I walked out with Ash. "Give it five minutes," I said.

The couple was out in three.

The next morning, I spoke to Detective Mackenzie, who got together a small team. To make myself feel better, I left Ash behind at the station and led the team through the dimensional portal. I know they thought it was all very weird, to be outfitted in SWAT gear and stepping into and through a closet.

Their lieutenant didn't like the looks of it. The whole compound was fortified by an army. Plus, they didn't know if they had jurisdiction here.

So they did nothing.

By the time they decided to get the Feds involved, the portal had closed.

Ash had lost a week of school … and for what? Nothing. Well, not *nothing*. He got to see first-hand what it was like to deal with bureaucracy and the government -- and to learn that they were worthless.

However, I knew if it was just me, I probably would have been stuck in that dimension — if not killed there. So maybe, just maybe, Ash saved my life.

It wouldn't be the first time.

ABOUT THE AUTHOR

Find out more about the world of L. A. Jacob at *Grimaulkin's Grimoire* (grimaulkin.com) and *Dark Mystic Quill* (darkmysticquill.com).

YOU MIGHT ALSO ENJOY

Grimaulkin

by L. A. Jacob

*Treading the straight and narrow is not natural
to one who summons demons.*

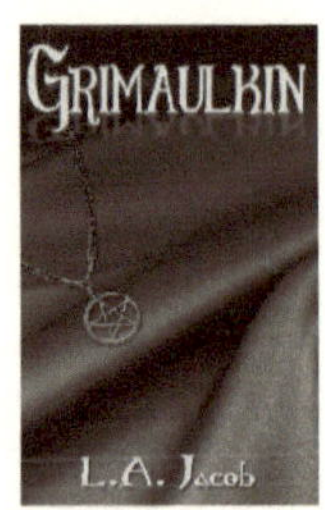

Grimaulkin Tempted

by L. A. Jacob

*Stress affects people differently. Then, there's
magic.*

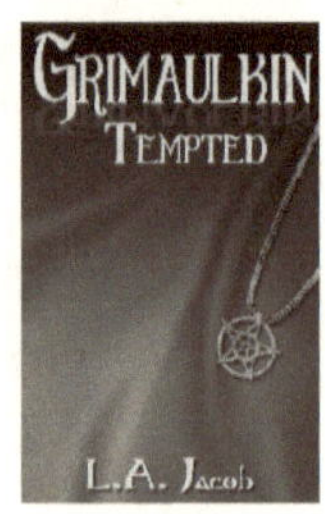

Grimaulkin Redeemed

by L. A. Jacob

Protect your present or suffer from your past.

Available from Paper Angel Press
in hardcover, trade paperback, digital, and audio editions
paperangelpress.com